a sweet sports holiday romance

PRESLEY'S CHRISTMAS CATCH

RANEÉ S. CLARK

To the fans who have been with me since "Playing for Keeps." You're the reason I can keep writing football romance. 🤍

CHAPTER 1
PRESLEY

June: The Wedding

I'm rethinking my decision to wear head-to-toe black to a wedding.

I don't think I look like I was dressing for a funeral—the wide-leg trousers are lightweight and flowy, and the sleeveless lace top is flirty. The heels I'm wearing don't look funeral appropriate either.

Listen, what I was going for was professional. Presley Tatum, physical therapist for the LA Rays football team. I'm honored that the star running back for the Rays, Lincoln Knight, invited me to his wedding. And I enjoy the camaraderie I feel with the players on the team, but as a member of the Rays training staff, there's a certain distance I feel like I should keep with them. When players get too close to team staff like me, it's asking for trouble. I thought not wearing a party dress while I was, well, partying with them might help me remember that in case the boundaries got a little blurry.

I didn't think about how Lincoln obviously knows guys from other teams who are really good-looking, and I don't need to keep a boundary with them. Like the New York Empire backup quarterback who used to play for the Rays, or another receiver

Lincoln played with in college who's with the Cobras right now. Now I wish I was wearing a fun party dress with glitter or sparkles or … Something that made me feel more like a girl these guys might ask out, like the handful of actresses Layla invited. Every single one of them looks like they could have walked a red carpet to get here. The football players here are never going to notice me. They're much more likely to want to dance with a woman at this wedding who looks like she's here to have fun, not the one who dressed "professional."

My gaze flits to Brock Hunter, an old teammate of Lincoln's from college. He's a left-tackle for the Denver Devils, not the type of guy to get a lot of notice, the way Lincoln and the Rays quarterback, Eli Dash, do. Except Brock's temper on the field has made him famous. I snicker to myself as I think about the latest meme I came across of him, throwing his helmet to the ground and it bouncing back up at him. He bats it away and then kicks it. The caption was something about trying to avoid responsibility.

"I see you eyeing Brock," a voice says, surprising me. Lincoln's new wife, Layla, is at my side.

"Me? No. I'm not really into guys with tempers like his." I smile to soften the statement. Lincoln and Brock are good friends, and Lincoln mentioned last week, when the guys were in the facility for some off-season therapy, that Brock was coming to town early to help with the wedding. Their friendship has never made sense to me, considering what a big cinnamon roll Lincoln is, but football brings a lot of guys from different walks of life together.

"Ask your dad about him," Layla says. "He knows that Brock isn't anything like what the media portrays." My eyebrows arch up, which makes her smile widen. "Yeah, he's passionate. You, of all people, know the intensity these guys have to live at to go pro in a sport like football."

I study Brock again. He's dancing alongside Eli Dash's wife and grinning like he's having the time of his life, which, yeah, feels a little off considering his reputation. "Maybe," I say. "But still."

She puts a hand on my elbow. "Listen, Presley, there are plenty of good-looking players for you to flirt with." She winks at me, and I chuckle. I *have* been scoping out my options. "Don't dismiss Brock because of what the media and the commentators say. The Devils are creating a narrative, and making Brock out to be the football bad-guy distracts people from the real problems there."

That's true. The Devils had the worst record in the league last season, and it doesn't look like things are going to get better this year. My dad, a former Rays football player, has commented on the poor coaching.

She squeezes my elbow. "I'm saying he's a good guy." We look up to see Lincoln waving her over. She gives my elbow one more squeeze and dances towards him. I can't help glancing at Brock again, still dancing with Court Dash. Even she wouldn't be out of place on the red carpet. Was there a red carpet walk to the wedding that I missed? Maybe only for the high-profile guests.

Brock's smile is not a thing football fans see a lot, which backs up what Layla said. Sports channels and social media do focus on his brooding side, the guy who has a reputation for speaking his mind, even if his opinion gets him in trouble. In the sports world, Brock Hunter gets clicks when he glares or throws something on the sideline.

They clearly haven't discovered this smile. Because he's straight-up gorgeous when he smiles. That, combined with Layla's words, make me curious about him and what else I don't know that wouldn't jive with his reputation.

His eyes meet mine, surprising me. Also embarrassing me, because I've been caught ogling him, but I try to own it by smiling at him. His gaze drops to the necklace my aunt gave me a couple years ago, and he squints then scowls.

Um, okay.

So there's the Brock Hunter we all know. He might be a great guy like Layla says, but I'm going to need more proof. I quickly turn away and feel twice as self-conscious about my dancing as before. Maybe I can seek out an actor friend of Layla's instead. I like football players fine, especially since I work around a lot of them. But I don't have a type or anything.

I scout the people around me dancing. The easiest way to strike up a conversation with someone would be slowly dancing my way over like it's an accident. Weddings are the perfect time to find dates, and I don't want to be left out. All I'm asking for is the number of a nice, good-looking guy. Besides, Aunt Shannon would be proud of me for putting myself out there. I've never been shy, but I've definitely tried harder the last year to take more chances.

"Hi!" a voice says loudly over the music, making me spin around. Brock Hunter stands behind me, hands in his pockets, and his expression … well, he's not glaring, but he's not laughing like he was with Court, either. Not even a smirk. Like I said, he's not known for his cheery attitude, so I try to ignore the discomfort his unreadable face conveys and remember what Layla said about him.

"Uh, hi," I call back, nodding at him and smiling. I can't help it. I'm a nervous smiler, and he makes me very nervous. The white lights strung along the ceiling of the tent twinkle in his dark brown eyes, but the firm set of his lips make sure I don't fall for the trick of light and mistake him for happy.

Brock is also huge. I'm used to big football players, I am. I work on them all the time. But somehow his height—well over Lincoln's six foot four—seems overwhelming. And for a left tackle, one of the guys directly responsible for protecting the quarterback, Brock is surprisingly slim. I mean, he's not actually slim. He probably weighs something like 275, but linemen are usually hefty-looking. Brock looks like he could run a five forty.

But also like he could stop a car coming at him by lowering his shoulders.

He has his hands in the pockets of his dress pants. His suit is black, his white dress shirt pristine, and as one of Lincoln's groomsmen, his yellow tie matches the wedding colors.

He nods toward my necklace and says something.

"I'm sorry, what?" I shout back.

He steps closer but also raises his voice. "I like your necklace. Where did you get it?"

My fingers automatically find the silly black stone etched with the crest of a fake kingdom from a book series I loved when I was a kid.

Okay, fine. Yes, I reread the whole series last year.

Heat dumps into my cheeks, and I wonder why Brock would fixate on this. Up against the black of my outfit, I didn't think anyone would even notice it. Otherwise I would have chosen something a little more elegant for a wedding.

This necklace *looks* elegant, though. And I thought Aunt Shannon would have gotten a kick out of me wearing it to something like this.

Ugh, I miss her, and it's stupid that Brock just asking about my necklace has tears stinging the backs of my eyes.

"My aunt gave it to me." I move closer to him to be heard. My voice breaks a little, but I think that's from having a conversation at high volume. I hope. "It's from a book I like." Books, actually. Fifteen of them. *Should* be sixteen, but Gideon Thornridge has been silent on that subject for over ten years now.

Brock smirks.

And there I go again. That smile softens him so much—and, of course, makes me weak in the knees. Flashing it at me should be considered a dangerous weapon.

"The Obsidian Kingdom," he says.

I blink rapidly in shock. Brock Hunter knows about The Obsidian Kingdom book series? No one knows about this book series. Not really.

His smile widens, and even if he was about to make fun of me for what might be a silly thing to still be obsessed with at nearly thirty years old, I wouldn't even care. I'm telling you, this smile is the thing of legends.

"Let's get something to drink," he suggests, nodding toward the open bar.

I follow, unsure where this is going and how it relates to TOK, as us fans like to refer to the beloved series. All one hundred of us.

Is Brock Hunter one of those one hundred? I bite back amusement at the thought. Probably not, but maybe someone he knows.

I order a Coke from the bar since I'm not much of a drinker, and Brock follows suit, then leads me toward a table away from the dance floor, where it's a lot quieter.

"I've read TOK about a dozen times," he says when we stop at the table.

I nearly miss my chair as I move to sit down. Brock grabs my arm and keeps me up, all while steadying my Coke on the table. "Sorry," I murmur, slipping into my chair. "I'm not really used to anyone knowing about TOK." The fact that he's read it as many times as I have convinces me more than anything that he's the good guy Layla said he is.

"There are only a few of us," he says dryly. His smile has faded, but amusement lines his expression.

I chuckle. "Very rare to stumble into another fan."

He looks down at my necklace again, his lips turning up ever so slightly. "I read the first one for a middle school parent-kid reading thing." His expression tenses the slightest bit and then relaxes. "Couldn't help but read all the rest."

I put my elbows on the table and lean forward. "Parent-kid reading thing?"

"Didn't your school do something like that?" he asks. "You had to pick an adult to read a book with and discuss it? Then they had to sign a paper saying you'd done it for a grade."

"Not that I can remember. But it sounds fun." I'm seeing a little bit of the passion Layla was talking about. There's excitement in his eyes that probably mirrors my expression—eagerness in finding someone to share something you love with. The football players I know—my dad, the team members I work with, especially the ones I can call friends—they're all passionate about the sport they love.

He looks down at the table. "It was good for me," he says in a low voice. I barely catch it with all the background noise, and I instinctively lean in closer then catch myself and sit back again. "How about you? How did you discover it?"

"My aunt bought the first one at a garage sale for me because she thought it looked like something I'd like." I was really into fantasy books as a kid. Read all the *Fablehaven* series and *Percy Jackson* and anything similar my library had. "I had to save all my babysitting money that summer to buy the rest of the series because my library didn't have them. Did yours?"

He gives a short laugh. "No. I grew up in a tiny Wyoming town. A family friend bought them for me." He shakes his head in a nostalgic way, a smile remaining. He's warming up to me a little, I think. "He's the one who suggested TOK," Brock goes on, "though I don't know how he came across it. Probably googled 'books with battle scenes for angry teenage boys to let off steam' or something."

I snort. Are his outbursts off the field something he's struggled with since he was younger? Maybe the family friend thought reading would simmer him down? I want to know more, and finding out that he's read a series I've been obsessed with since I was a teen flicks to life the spark of a crush.

I can picture Aunt Shannon eyeing me teasingly. She loved to rib me about my crushes and how freely I admitted to them, small or big. She was my best friend, so we talked about everything. She was the same with me, especially once I was out of high school. She didn't spare details about the men she dated, and when she met her boyfriend, Thomas, she confessed within days that she knew he was the one. She was practically vibrating with excitement the night she told me that they'd talked about their future for the first time and that Thomas hadn't been afraid to confess he knew they were headed for something serious.

Then her diagnosis took it all away.

I push those thoughts out, because tonight I am channeling the Aunt Shannon who wanted to find joy in every small moment, especially a few hours with a cute guy. "I heard there's going to be a sixteenth book. Soon maybe," I say.

Brock's expression brightens. "Yeah. I read somewhere that it could even drop as a surprise this summer."

Somewhere. The only place people talk about TOK are obscure Reddit threads or the TOK forum on the website. I wonder if I've ever seen him post something. That flicker of a crush flares. And besides that, this conversation is hard to fit with the memes that pop up of him throwing things. It makes me want to find out about the good guy Layla told me not to dismiss.

"I've heard that story before," I say. "I'm trying not to get my hopes up."

"Same." Brock takes a sip of his Coke. Our eyes meet for a moment, and it seems like he relaxes a little more into his seat. "Still, I can't help but cross my fingers. I'm dying to know if Lyra gave up her powers or took the chance that she could save Eldraeth with them."

I raise my eyebrows. "You're glossing over the biggest part of the choice—abandoning Kael."

Brock stares at me, that squinty, almost a glare, look coming back, but I see it for what it is now. He's pondering. He's one of those people who has a resting angry face, and it's been misunderstood. One side of his mouth turns up. "How could I forget?"

There's something knowing in that turn of his lips that makes me blush. Yes, as a thirteen-year-old girl, I was extremely invested in the romantic subplot of Lyra and Kael through the books.

Okay, yes. I still am.

Also, I have a feeling that next time I reread the books, how I imagine Kael to look might shift. He'll be impossibly tall, blond hair darkening closer to the roots, and a neatly trimmed beard and mustache.

Our conversation turns into discussion and light-hearted arguments over various plot lines and fan theories. Little by little, the grumpy persona Brock hides behind fades. I'm seeing the good guy that could be friends with Lincoln, that would have Layla championing him.

After our third Cokes, Brock nods to my necklace again. "Is your aunt a fan of the books too? You said she bought them for you."

I keep a smile on my face because even though Brock and I have solidly bonded over TOK, it's too soon to cry in front of him. Talking about Aunt Shannon doesn't always bring me to tears. It's been almost a year since she died. But even though she only read the first book with me, she supported my habit in every way she could. The only reason she didn't buy me the rest of the series from Amazon herself was because Mom insisted I should earn it.

"Not really," I say, grateful my voice is steady. I clear my throat to make sure it stays that way. "But she loved my obsession and fed it all the time."

"Loved." He catches the way I used past tense and tilts his head at me.

My smile turns into a sad one that I can't help. "She passed away almost a year ago." I reach up and touch the necklace. "She was my best friend."

"I'm sorry, Presley." The genuineness to his tone melts my insides.

"I think Layla might have been right," I murmur.

I can't believe he picks it up amidst all the noise around us, but his pondering face comes back as he eyes me. "Right about what?"

My cheeks warm, but I think of Aunt Shannon and how she'd be giving me eyebrow wiggles and encouraging me to flirt it up if she were here. "Just that you're a good guy, despite your penchant for helmet throwing."

He lets out a short, dry laugh. "Long story short, my dad left when I was eight, and my mom didn't have money for a therapist—not that I would've talked to one, to be honest—so she signed me up for football so I had an outlet for my anger. I know I shouldn't do stuff like that on the sidelines, that I should express my frustration in private. And that the Devils are using it to sweep stuff under the rug. But dumping a cooler of ice water out—" Oh, yeah. I'd forgotten about that meme last season. "It's better than me pointing out all the ways my teammates aren't doing their jobs." I barely catch it, but he says under his breath, "I know football." It's not meant for me to hear, and unlike him, I let it go because this is different than admitting that maybe Layla is trying to do some matchmaking. He's reassuring himself.

"Things are bad?" I say anyway. Honestly, anyone watching a few football games knows the Devils are in a spiral that no one wants to take responsibility for. Not management, not the coaches, and definitely not the all-stars they keep trading for to save the sinking ship.

It's a couple moments before he answers, and he doesn't meet my eye when he does. "Too many guys are in it for themselves, trying to be the star and to make the headlines. That's not how *teams* work." He looks up and meets my gaze. "McKay Thompson was picked in the first round, led LSU to a national championship. He's one of the best QBs in the league, but none of that matters if he doesn't have time to make plays, if linebackers are on top of him before he can hand off—forget about getting a pass. And if he does? Half the time it's intercepted because he has to rush it." He shakes his head quickly. "I'm sorry. You probably don't want to know all of that."

It's my turn to smirk, although I don't think it's as sexy as when Brock does it. There really is something to say about those brooding guys. And I have a weakness for them—thank you, Sir Kael Winteridge.

"You know who my dad is, right?"

"Hmm. Presley Tatum … Tatum." His eyes widen, surprised. "Wait. *That* Tatum? As in Steven Tatum, the legend?"

"I can't wait to tell him you said that." I grin. "The point is, I can talk football. And I like to. I wouldn't be working for the Rays if I didn't."

He returns my grin, and the way it lights up his face makes tiny footballs bounce around in my stomach. "Well, Presley, I don't know what it is about tonight. Maybe it's that you're a fellow TOK fan—" He makes the sign of the Eldraeth brotherhood, three fingers pressed against his heart. I giggle, which I try to reel in and then can't. "Or drinking all this soda," he continues. "But I've said more to you about all that than I've told anyone except Lincoln."

"You got a Veilstone on you?" I ask in a teasing voice. "I'll happily Shadowbind your secret and take it to my grave."

"Too bad. I'm fresh out. Any chance that necklace is a Veilstone?"

I pick it up and finger it. "Pretty sure it's glass. Or maybe a rock painted black." I shrug. Aunt Shannon showed me the Etsy store she got the necklace from, and the artist is legit, but I don't think they're charging $19.95 for real obsidian.

"Guess I'll just have to trust you." He makes a face like it's no big deal, but I don't buy it.

My arms tingle, but I try to ignore that my crush is snow-balling. He's a TOK fan—honestly, what more do I need in a man?—and that smile *is* something to write home about. The broody side of him is a mystery I want to solve, and if Layla Knight, the wife of the sweetest guy I know, says Brock is a keeper, I can't help but trust her.

The truth is I think Brock might be my real-life version of Kael.

Aunt Shannon would have approved.

CHAPTER 2
BROCK

I head to my hometown of Little River, Wyoming after the wedding to spend time with my mom until I have to go back to Denver for one of the mini training camps the Devils will do before full training starts in July.

Presley Tatum and I text regularly after the wedding, almost entirely about TOK. I've been around the forums, and there are a lot of people that know the ins and outs of the book—like me—but it's weird to discuss them with someone in person. Someone I can put a name and a face to.

Someone other than Tim, my old coach and the family friend who did the parent-kid reading thing with me back in middle school.

I'm sitting out on my mom's spacious deck, enjoying the view of the sunrise over the mountains because I'm an early riser, and sipping on a protein shake. I'll have a more substantial breakfast later, but this is my morning pick-me up. The temperature is perfect, not hot like it will be later in the day, but a nice sixty-five-degree mountain morning.

Little River, Wyoming is close to Denver, relatively speaking, only about six hours by car. My mom was thrilled when I was traded from the Pumas four and a half years ago—definitely more thrilled than me, since I'd be so close to her.

I clench my fists as I think about how much I wish I was still playing for the Pumas. It was nothing personal for me. They were trading for a player they needed to fit in their system, and I guess I hadn't proven myself yet. What I wouldn't give to be back on a team that valued creating a cohesive atmosphere like that.

I sigh and massage my temples. I need to push football and all the troubles on the Devils out of my mind for at least the time I'm here with Mom. If I don't give myself some "off" time, I'm going to explode this year for sure. I've come too far and worked too hard to do that.

I stare out at the green around me—farmers' fields and the trees that climb up into the mountains. It's quiet here. Every once in a while there's a rumble from a car on the distant highway, but it's mostly just birds chirping this morning. It's peaceful, and I focus on the birdsong and the whisper of the breeze.

My phone buzzes with a text, drawing me out of my thoughts. Mom is already at work, taking an early shift at the local hospital, and she's the only person I text regularly that's up this early. Even though I bought her this house, and I'm more than happy to support her since she worked her tail off supporting me after my dad left, she can't stay still.

Presley: We should reread all the books. Like a Presley and Brock book club.

We've both read them so many times, but it would be fun to read again with a friend. Like when Tim read the first one with me back then but better because it would be all of them. I'm not embarrassed about loving TOK the way I do, maybe because it's tied into one of the few good things from my childhood. That's why I didn't have any issue with walking up to Presley and asking her about her necklace when I recognized the crest from TOK. But I don't go around broadcasting my love for those books either.

Maybe I should. It might be a better headline than all the stupid posts and memes about my temper that are all played up for an image. Besides, it's not as bad as it always comes off in the press. I say something stupid about a play in the heat of the moment and then regret it because we're all trying our best. Then everyone twists it like I blamed someone for the bad play, and they frame it like I'm pro-football's villain.

It's fine. I've made my peace with being that guy.

Mostly.

I send an answer to Presley.

Brock: It would be perfect timing for the new one to come out this summer.

She sends a GIF of a skeleton waiting.

Presley: We could only be so lucky, Brock.

I suck up the last of the protein shake and stare out at the mountains for a couple minutes longer before getting up to make breakfast. A few more texts come in while I'm cooking but I focus on the meal. Offensive linemen like me don't stay this size by accident, and it's not all about gorging myself, either. It's about healthy calories with a lot of protein. When I sit down with my eggs, protein waffles, and bacon, I enjoy the view of the valley where Little River is nestled out of Mom's floor-to-ceiling windows on one wall of the dining room. She doesn't get to be outside a lot with her busy nursing schedule, and big windows to let in the beautiful scenery around her country home was one of her only requests when we built the house.

I finally check my phone in case it's something important. Could be a text from the team or my agent that I need to address. One is from Tim, my first football coach. The guy my mom says was exactly what I needed to get my head on straight after my dad left. Tim was a lot more than that too. Did the surrogate dad thing the best he could. I basically grew up with his boys, Chase and Derek, which is why he's the one who volunteered to do the reading thing with me when Mom didn't have ten minutes of free time together between her shifts as a nurse and trying to raise me.

Tim: Football camp starts for the boys this week. Want to come work out? Six p.m. at the high school.

Tim graduated from my little league football coach to a state-championship winning high school coach by the time his boys and I had reached high school. We won two state championships when I was a junior and a senior, and he's won five more since. I'll work out on my own first, but helping Tim and working out with the boys sounds fun. I send a thumbs-up confirming I'll be there and then open the other text, which is from Lincoln.

Lincoln: Trying not to hover, but you never told me how things are going with Presley.

I scowl at the text. How things are going? What's that supposed to mean? I told him that I enjoyed hanging out with her, and Lincoln knows about how much I love TOK. You don't spend three years on a football team with someone and not learn a few secrets. Plus, like I said, I'm not embarrassed. My special collector's edition set, a gift from Tim when I graduated from high school with a full ride to USC, was on proud display on a shelf above my bed in my dorm room, and then in my bedroom at the house I lived in with Lincoln and a few other guys.

I palm my face.

Lincoln's now a proud member of Eli Dash's Former Best Friends Club, and he probably thinks that because I spent a couple hours laughing with Presley at his wedding it means I like her. Ugh. Matchmaking is about to commence. I feel it, even from over a thousand miles away.

Brock: DO NOT get your club involved in this. I'm just friends with Presley. For real. We talked about books that whole time.

That's not entirely a lie. We did talk *mostly* about the books, but our conversation touched on other topics, like her aunt and the Devils. But Lincoln will definitely read into me confiding in her about my frustrations. It was easy to talk to Presley, and the fact that we live so far apart made telling her stuff about my poor relationship with my teammates feel like not that big of a deal.

Lincoln: Club?
Brock: Don't act innocent. I know what this is. You and Dash meddling. It's not like that.
Lincoln: Bro. Friends is the best way to start.
Brock: Linc. I'm serious. I don't feel that way about her and I don't want you leading her on or whatever by making it seem like this is something it's not.

Presley is sweet, and I enjoyed our conversation. I don't want Lincoln messing that up, even if he has good intentions. Sure, Presley is beautiful, but things are totally platonic between us. It sounds cliché, but she's not my type. She's cheerful and fun, the opposite of my intensity. Even when she talked briefly about her aunt and how she passed away suddenly last year, her voice was light as she told me about her. That's definitely not me. While the angry, brooding image the media's painted of me is exaggerated, it's not wrong. Besides, in all the texts between us, she's never given me any indication that she's into me either. No flirting. No comments that have double meaning. None of that.

Lincoln: Okay, okay. Guess I misread the situation.

He sends a gif of a guy holding his hands up in surrender, and I breathe a sigh of relief.

Brock: Thanks.

I clean up after myself in the kitchen, changing the water in a vase of daisies my mom's boyfriend sent a couple days ago. Guys who are in love do stuff like that, the way my mom's boyfriends have over the years.

I've had no desire to send Presley flowers, fyi. I consider texting Lincoln that, but he's already surrendered, and I don't want to bring it up again. He'll make it a thing.

I head to the basement and the home gym. Mom uses it sometimes, but it was mostly me adding it in to the plans to make visiting her for stretches of time like this easier. She's a runner and prefers running the trails around here when the weather permits.

An hour later, after my shower, I send Presley another text with a picture of me and my old, highlighted, creased, and dog-eared copy of *The Obsidian Kingdom*, the first book in the series.

Brock: Starting now. Go!
Presley: Not fair! You don't have to work.
Brock: 😂 Your schedule is light too. Don't try and hustle me.
Presley: 😈

She sends a picture of her own very worn version of the book. Somehow I know this is the copy her aunt bought her all those years ago, and I like thinking that, without even saying anything to each other, we both chose to start this with our OG books. I grin. I've never gotten to share TOK with someone like this in real life, only in online conversations with people I've never met. It's cool.

Presley: Already to chapter ten, sucker!

I laugh out loud. Oh, it's on.

CHAPTER 3
PRESLEY

Brock is right that I have a lot of time on my hands right now, and I'm taking advantage of it. When training camp starts in July, my busy football season schedule will start along with it, so I'm enjoying the weeks I have where things are chill. As a training staff, we do have some players coming in over their time off for us to keep tabs on older injuries. For example, right now we have a wide receiver who had ankle surgery at the end of last season, and we're rehabbing him and hoping he's going to be back by the time we have our first regular season game in September.

The point is that I'm already halfway through the first book and I just barely suggested this to Brock yesterday. I'd feel weird about maybe getting into this more than him except he texted me fifteen minutes ago with a quote that tells me he's not far behind.

My back is starting to cramp from lying on my bed half the day reading this book, so I set it aside, confident I can still stay ahead of Brock, and go in search of book two from my old collection. I love the idea of rereading with Brock, and okay, maybe I have this notion of us falling in love through our mutual obsession with this series, and I'm hoping to kick-start that with reading it together. But part of the reason I'm reading my old copy is for Aunt Shannon. I miss her so much, and something about reading the book she gave me helps me feel close to her. I can picture her face when she handed me the book, all hopeful, and the grin when my eyes widened at the cover. It has this dreamy look to it—Lyra with big doe eyes and a creamy complexion whited out by an orbed light in her hands, her brown hair swirling around her with some unknown, magical wind. And Kael, dark haired and brooding in the background. Thirteen-year-old me had a crush on him before I even cracked the already cracked spine. I judged that book by its cover, obviously, and fell in love with the story before I even read a word.

Aunt Shannon read the book that summer, right after I did, and promised me it was the best thing she'd ever read. Looking back, I remember that gleam in her eyes and the crooked smile, and I can interpret how she agreed with me because I was her favorite niece. (Okay, yeah, her only niece.) And we were buddies. She got me. Despite being close to my mom, I had a bond with Aunt Shannon that was a "just us girls" kind of thing.

Right up to the day she died, I told her all about all my crushes, about every guy I thought was cute, and every detail about my relationships, long or short, including the kissing. She probably relayed all of it to Mom, but it didn't matter. She was my bestie.

I'm rooting around the top shelf of my closet, looking for book two, which is mysteriously not with the rest of my collection on a bookcase in my room, when my gaze lands on the small, shoebox-size storage container Aunt Shannon left me when she died. It's been almost a year, and I haven't been able to look into it yet. I grab it and step down from the step stool, holding it carefully in both hands as I walk to my bed. Tears immediately well in my eyes, and I almost take it back, but what happened with Brock last week has given me new courage. I think Aunt Shannon would have been disappointed that I've been this scared to open it.

"It's not that, Shan," I say out loud. My voice cracks. I swipe a tissue from the nightstand next to my bed. "Once I open this, that's it. There's nothing more." And she's gone. Forever. As long as the stuff in this box stays there, I still have things about Aunt Shannon to discover. Once I open it, they're just memories, like everything else I have left of her.

I stare down at the box, telling myself I'm gonna do it. I'm going to open the box.

Aunt Shannon had ALS, and it took her from us when she was only forty-eight. When I was younger, she always felt so much older than me, but now that I'm almost thirty, forty-eight feels a lot younger, just around the corner. The day after she got the diagnosis, she started putting stuff together in these little storage containers for everyone close to her: Mom, Dad, me, and her boyfriend, Thomas. Mom had snort-laughed when she opened hers the day after the funeral and found a pile of sticky notes with furniture and clothing items listed that Aunt Shannon wanted her to have but was still using. When I couldn't look in mine right away, I told Mom to open it so she could gather up the stuff Aunt Shannon wanted me to have: the LA Rays hoodie I'd given her for Christmas the year I got the training job with the Rays and a few items of jewelry. The hoodie is in my closet. I shoved the jewelry into the box and closed the lid back up. Thomas asked Mom to do it for him too. He couldn't bear to go through her stuff, to see any of it. It was hard to lose Aunt Shannon so quickly. It was also hard to see how much her death shattered the man who loved her.

Now I put my hand on the lid and rest it there. Then I laugh. "I'm acting like your ashes are in here." I lift the lid without further ado. Like I'm pulling off Kinesio tape quickly from an athlete because it's funny to see those big guys flinch at such a little thing.

I set aside the tangled jewelry I put in there a year ago and sift through the box. There's a small notebook with a floral cover, full of Aunt Shannon's handwriting—they look like quotes. I flip absently through the pages, knowing if I stop on any one that I won't make it through looking at anything else in this box. There's a thick envelope with my name on the outside. The flap isn't sealed shut, and inside is a stack of folded papers.

The first one is labeled, *Open on your 30th birthday*. The others are similar: *When you meet "The One," When you get married, When you have your first baby, On your fortieth birthday*, and one that nearly undoes me, *When your mom dies*.

I shuffle *When you meet "The One"* to the front of the pile, indulging in the warmth swirling in my chest in hope that maybe it's happened. Brock and I are just texting. I have a crush, yes, one that's growing day by day as we text. Maybe it could turn into something?

I stuff them all back in their envelope and set them aside. There are a few trinkets she collected from trips with me. One is a keychain with "Pumas" written in vintage script from when she came to Houston to see the Rays play them at Christmas a couple years ago. She crashed at my hotel with me, and it's a memory I still treasure since she died a year later. There's a picture in a frame of us at Disney World right after I graduated from high school. Aunt Shannon took me to celebrate my last moments of freedom, she called them, before I went to college and started the grueling undergrad program for my path to PT school.

My phone dings, and I welcome the interruption. Opening the box is as heavy as I suspected it would be, even if the memories all warm me. Even if I'm grateful that Aunt Shannon took the time to put all this together to help me remember her. To help me remember the good life we had together, as short as it was.

Brock: I'm seeing Lyra's first betrayal with new eyes. Hear me out. What if the big reveal in the last book is her identity …
Brock: The Obsidian Queen

I snort. Lyra would never. I return the items I've left out on the bed to the box and put the lid back on to sort through more later. For now I need a break.

Presley: No other reason a woman would have that much power except to take over the world.
Brock: No, no, no.
Brock: #girlpower and all that.
Brock: Just saying it would be the biggest twist.
Presley: Pretty much everyone agrees that Seren Moonvale is the Obsidian Queen.
Brock: Too easy.
Presley: Simplest answer is usually the right one.
Brock: She's literally cursed from the dark magic of the Obsidian Kingdom.
Presley: Or so she says …
Brock: 😂
Presley: Lyra has had to do some bad things, yes. But she would never, EVER kill Kael's brother. That's unforgiveable. Kael and Lyra 4evah.

Brock responds with a GIF of a woman snort laughing and almost spitting out her drink, and I grin at the thought that I might have made him react like that.

Brock: Maybe The Obsidian Queen is misunderstood. Maybe there's something else going on here.
Presley: If only there was a sixteenth book.

He sends a link to a new article I haven't seen yet. An anonymous source is claiming that they have a friend who was an editor on the rumored sixteenth book who can't talk about it, but the book is definitely coming out this year.

Presley: Seems sketchy. Friend of a friend?

Brock: Playing the heartstrings of poor, devoted fans. If it's legit, the leak was planned. I guarantee it.

Presley:

Brock: Already at the throne room battle scene. You?

The throne room? That's nearly three-quarters through the book. I glance over at my nightstand, where I'd laid down my open book at page 175, not even halfway through. The first book is by far the shortest in the series. If Brock beats me through this one, I'll never catch up.

Presley: Psh. Almost done, rookie.

I smirk at the lie, but I have all night, and Brock is an early riser. (Too many texts at five a.m. for my taste, even if they are from him.)

Brock:

Presley: Shhh, please. Reading.

I grab my book and my phone, splurging by opening the QuickEats app so I won't have to waste time figuring out food. By the time I'm settled comfortably on my couch, book in hand, my late lunch is on its way.

CHAPTER 4
BROCK

I don't know why I'm so intent on beating Presley through book one, but I almost don't go down to football camp like I told Tim I would. I mean, I didn't say I was going to be there. Just gave him a thumbs up, which could totally mean that I got the message.

But spending all day reading isn't something I've done for years, not since before college, and I'm antsy by the time six rolls around. Working out with the high schoolers will be the break I need. I can order a quick dinner from the diner for me and Mom to pick up on my way home and get a couple more hours of reading in after she goes to bed. With her early shifts, she'll be asleep by eight.

Tim's grandson, Mason, runs up to me when I walk onto the field where the team is stretching out and chatting in small groups. Tim's son, Chase, got married right out of high school and had a baby right away with his high school sweetheart. Mason has been following Tim around to football practices and games since he was little. The twelve-year-old gives me a high-five when I walk up. He's just starting to grow, shooting up to five foot six and proud of it. He measures himself next to me, like he does every time he sees me.

"Getting close to your shoulder," he claims.

I hold back a laugh. I'm still well over a foot taller, but I'm not going to burst his bubble. "Any day now, bro."

A few kids on the team wave or call out to me from where they're stretching. I've been coming to their camps and summer stuff for a while, so they're comfortable. The younger kids stare, and I'm never sure if it's because of my size or because they know who I am. Left tackles aren't usually the guys who get the glory on ESPN, although I have gotten my fair share of press, thanks to the power of memes.

I stop by where Kaden Jacobs is stretching out his arms, and he pauses to hold out his fist to bump mine. "Kaden, impressive," I say, eyeing the way he's bulked up since last year.

He grins. This will be his second year starting center for the team, and it's obvious he's taking that seriously. He must have gained thirty pounds since I saw him last, most of it muscle. "Did everything you told me to. Looked up that meal plan and stuff. U-Dub wants me to commit."

I slap him on the shoulder. "And?" I ask. University of Wyoming could definitely use an athlete like Kaden.

"There are other schools interested, so we'll see." He wipes at his forehead with his shirt, already sweating even though the workout hasn't even started. It's hot, hovering over eighty, and the sun won't set for another couple hours, so no relief in sight.

The eagerness in Kaden's eyes sparks excitement in my chest. I remember when the colleges first started calling when I was a junior, UW among them. It was the first time I felt like I was accomplishing my goals.

"Kaden. That's awesome."

"INCOMING!"

I hear the shout only seconds before arms wrap around my waist and someone attempts to throw me to the ground. I do stumble since the attack took me by surprise and because I'm laughing so hard.

"Ugh." Colby Sutton shakes his head in disgust as he steps

back. "I thought the element of surprise was on my side this time."

"You almost had me." I size up the sophomore safety and receiver. In a small town like Little River, a lot of the boys play both defense and offense. "The good news is that most of the receivers you'll be tackling won't be nearly three-hundred pounds. Also, try double-teaming me with Cade next time. Could work," I say, nodding toward his twin, who's strolling up behind him. The boys rib Colby for thinking he could actually tackle me. I'm still chuckling when I approach Tim, who stands about ten yards away from where all the boys are warming up.

"Ready for training camp?" Tim asks when I reach him.

"Yeah, enjoying my time here though. Where everything is a lot simpler." Get up. Work out. Read books. Hang out with my mom. See some of the guys from high school. Enjoy the way the air is crisp and clear here and smells fresh. I've never doubted that I'm retiring back here someday.

"You're looking really good, Brock. Remember that," he says. The familiar dad-tone in his voice makes me believe it. I wish he was on staff with the Devils. My temper would be a lot easier to handle. It helped in high school that Tim always knew exactly what to say or when to sit me down because I was about to boil over. He's known me most of my life, almost like a dad, so it makes sense that he can read me like that. I don't know the Devils coaches as well, and it makes things harder.

I thought when I grew up the world would seem more fair. Like the farther I got from my dad leaving, the easier it would be. But more frustrations are always in the wings, pushing at me until I'm overwhelmed, and it all comes spilling out. Sometimes with a hard tackle that people comment on or me throwing my helmet on the sidelines. Sometimes with me running my mouth to reporters. And with the last few seasons with the Devils being frustrating for everyone, a lot of stuff is pent up.

But I'm trying hard to be the cool, calm guy that Tim is. I

want him to be proud of me. Besides, I owe him. He sacrificed so much time for me when he didn't have to.

"Are you having fun still?" he asks.

I let out a short combo of a laugh and frustrated huff. "It's hard when things are the way they are."

He folds his arms, his contemplative expression showing me how seriously he takes my feelings on this. "Yeah. I can see the disconnect when you're out there." He lets out a sigh. "Having fun is important at any level, even with the pressure you're under. You gotta figure out a way to find the enjoyment again."

Easier said than done, and he knows it. I don't have to point it out. I move back toward the kids to stretch out with them and help Tim instruct.

An hour later, as we're starting to run some offensive plays with the team, Tim's wife pulls up. I hide my smile as his eyes follow her when she hops out of her Tahoe and makes her way toward the field. Even after thirty-five years together, he can't keep his eyes off her if she's anywhere nearby. When I was in high school and spending a lot of time at their house with Chase and Derek, we used to tease them for how affectionate they were, but in truth, even then, their loving marriage was a comfort to me.

"You got the boys for a second while I see what Meg needs?" Tim doesn't wait for my assent before he walks to meet her by the bleachers. He kisses her as soon as they greet, and the boys wolf whistle and holler until I call them back to order, grinning myself at two fifty-somethings acting like teenagers.

The workout is easier than my normal ones, but it's a great distraction. It's also a great reminder of what Tim's talking about —having fun. I step in on more than a few plays to "instruct" the guys on stuff. And sure, it's easy when I'm blocking kids half my size and all that's on the line is bragging rights for who wins the scrimmage. (My team, of course.) But it reminds me of the love for the game I've had since I first put on a helmet. My friends like Lincoln and Jett McCombs are playing for good teams and having the time of their lives, by the looks of it. I can't control the team I'm on, or even how the rest of the line behaves—whether they protect our quarterback with all their heart or are only looking out for their own career. But I can control how hard I work. And if I have anything to say about it, nobody is getting around me.

———

Presley: Yes! Done! Beat you!
Brock: Noooo. I knew I shouldn't have gone to the football camp.
Presley: Camp? You guys still doing OTAs? Thought you'd get a break before training camp starts.
Brock: No, not with the Devils. I'm visiting my mom, and the high school coach here is a good friend. Hanging out with them.
Presley: I bet they love that.
Brock: They're teenagers. If they love it, they don't show it. Not most of them.
Presley: Did any of them fall out of their chairs when you started talking to them?
Brock: I thought that was because I knew about TOK.
Presley: I mean, it was. But my point remains.
Brock: The guys are cool. At least they act like it when I'm around. I've been coming to these camps for a while, so a lot of them know me and are used to me.
Presley: It sounds like fun. I bet the coach loves it too, being able to show you as an example of his success.
Brock: Tim's proud of me, no doubt.
Brock: But I think he's never going to be able to stop coaching me.
Presley: Tim sounds amazing. That's how my dad is, even though I don't play sports competitively anymore. He's still always trying to give me tricks from the PTs he liked that were with the team back when he played.

Brock: Tim will text me after games with a compliment, something I can improve, and then another compliment.
Brock: Same way he always coached.
Presley: The compliment sandwich!
Brock: 😂
Brock: Sometimes I think, in the long run, I was lucky my real dad left. Because I got Tim.
Presley: What about your real dad? Does he ever text you advice?
Brock: He'd have to know I grew up.
Presley: You don't talk to him?
Presley: Sorry, if you don't want to talk about him, that's fine.
Brock: Classiest thing that guy ever did was to not try to have a relationship with me after I made it to the pros.
Brock: No. We never talk. I don't even know where he is.
Brock: Honestly, I don't think I want to.
Presley: He'd probably be a disappointment after Tim.
Brock: No doubt.
Brock: I owe Tim so much. Even today, he's still trying to help me. Telling me to remember why I play and why I enjoy it, even when things aren't going great.
Brock: And being around the kids, who have all these big dreams, it keeps MY dreams alive. You know?
Presley: Sometimes remembering who we wanted to be when we could be anything is good for the soul.

I'm SITTING on the porch that evening, book open in my lap but distracted by texting Presley and also by an amazing sunset being painted in the sky in front of me. Gorgeous shades of pink and orange slashed through with faint white puffs of distant clouds, and the mountains almost purple in the gathering darkness. My texting conversation with Presley has me thinking about our conversation the night of the wedding and the sense of trust I had in her that came so quickly.

Instead of responding to her text about dreaming big being good for the soul, I click over and start a facetime call.

She answers quickly, her expression bright. "Brock! Hey!"

"Got a second to chat?" It seems dumb to ask. She wouldn't have picked up if she didn't, but assuming feels like a jerk move too.

"Of course." She pushes back a piece of hair that's falling in her face from the riotous messy bun on top of her head. I should screenshot this and send it to Lincoln—further proof that there's nothing between us but friendship. If she liked me romantically, she wouldn't have answered like this. In fact, in all the facetime calls I've had with girlfriends or potential girlfriends over the years, I can't remember one in the early days like this where the women didn't look put together, trying to impress me.

"I know this is just an attempt to delay me from starting the next book," she goes on, "but if anything, it's flattering that you're so threatened by my reading prowess."

Laughter bursts from me, the way it has multiple times when we text. "I have no ulterior motives, except I wanted to show you my view right now—something I guarantee you're not seeing in LA." I flip my camera around to pan the view before me, making sure to include my mom's picturesque porch with the swing as well as the comfy deck furniture I'm lounging in.

She sucks in a breath. "Oh, Brock …! It's gorgeous." There's a pause, and in the small square in the corner of my screen, I see her eyes moving over the picture, taking it in. "Beach sunsets are awesome in their own right, but this is something else."

I flip the screen back around, warmth in my chest at her appreciating one of my favorite views. When I make her the center of my screen again, I notice the way her eyes shimmer.

"Presley?" I furrow my brow. "Is everything okay?" The view wasn't *that* good.

She chuckles nervously and swipes at her eyes with her fingers. "Oh my gosh, Brock. Of course you're one of those guys who isn't bothered by the idea of tears so you pretend not to notice." She swipes again and sniffs. I think this is one of those times where the acknowledgement of her tears has encouraged them, but she's right. I'm okay if she needs to talk about something.

"Single mom," I remind her. "I'm comfortable with all sorts of things that lesser men fear—tampons, bras, UTIs? Come at me."

She gives me a look I can't interpret, maybe approval? "Hmmm." She turns around and then pulls a plastic storage container onto her lap, tilting her phone for me to see it. "My aunt left me this before she died. I finally had the courage to open it today."

My turn to suck in a breath. "Pres. That's a big deal."

She nods, her gaze on the box. "I was scared for a while, but not because I was afraid of being sad or grieving, you know? This is all I have left of her, and once I've seen it all, that's just …"

"It." I finish for her. "That's all there is."

"Yeah." She breathes the word.

I quirk an eyebrow. "Anything good?"

Her smile returns, and I'm reminded of the beaming sunshine she is to my stormy sky. "Letters from her to open at certain times."

"So … you still have more to discover."

She turns her gaze to the box again. "Yeah. Aunt Shan was cool like that."

Presley so easily discussing something difficult intrigues me. I don't purposely hold back about my dad leaving or how hard it was for my mom to make ends meet, but it's not easy for me to talk about either. I'm not saying that losing her aunt wasn't hard, but she makes it seem like she's good anyway. I need to learn from her. If I could take that attitude into playing for the Devils this season—I'm good anyway—it would temper some of my frustrations.

I settle back in my chair to observe her. "So, tell me all about her."

Presley leans back against the pillows on her bed, setting her box to the side and then adjusting to a comfortable position. "She left my mom a notebook full of stupid advice, like 'When in doubt, do the Hustle. Trust me on this.'"

"The Hustle?" I question, biting back a laugh.

She presses a hand to her forehead. "They were *sooo* bad at it, Brock."

"They were together a lot?"

"Inseparable."

"Well, I'm hoping you wrote down more of this great advice, because I could sure use advice in my life of any variety."

"I wrote all of it down in my notes app."

"Lay it on me."

CHAPTER 5
PRESLEY

Presley: I finally opened my box the other day. Didn't get all the way through it. But you're still proud of me, right?

Thomas: 🙌 You know there's no judgement here. There's an envelope in mine I haven't opened. A letter, I can tell, but I'm terrified of it.

Presley: I don't blame you. <gif of friends hugging>

I stare down at my phone as I sit in my car in the driveway at my parents' house. I texted Thomas this morning, but it's not surprising that it took him time to answer. His job keeps him busy. It wouldn't have been out of the ordinary if it had taken him several days. Sometimes I wonder if we'll all stop texting each other eventually, if there will be a time when Thomas doesn't feel like our family anymore. That's hard to picture.

My mom sits at the kitchen table with her laptop when I walk into her house. She turns to welcome me. "Hello, sweetie." She reaches out to grab my hand, and I squeeze it as I take a seat next to her.

"What are you up to?" I ask.

"Nothing. Wasting time. Mindlessly scrolling." She shrugs and pushes at her laptop, which is sitting in front of her. I catch a glimpse of a Facebook post with a close-up of an emerald ring with ruby stones flanking it almost like flower petals. The headline reads, "Is there a Christmas Miracle for a long-lost ring?"

"What's that about?" I gesture to the post she was looking at.

"Oh, you remember the ring that was stolen last year at the Westcott's big Christmas party?"

I furrow my brows at her. I remember the Christmas party. I go with my parents every year. The Westcotts have lived in the same neighborhood as my parents for as long as I can remember. Their daughter, Vivi, and I went to elementary school together, and Mrs. Westcott takes that to mean that my attendance is required with my parents, even though Vivi and I weren't close.

"A stolen ring?" I feel like I'd remember that.

Mom makes a face at me. "Presley. It's all Alexandra Westcott has talked about since it happened. You follow Vivi on Instagram, don't you?" she says.

"Yeah." But I can't remember the last time one of Vivi's posts came across my feed.

Mom waves her hand. "We were all there, Presley. They stopped the whole thing when they discovered it was gone, and refused to let anyone leave the house until they were searched. Thomas kept joking about having to explain to his bosses that he was under suspicion of burglary."

It hits me with a flash of Aunt Shannon's laughing face. The way she gave Thomas the side-eye but then grinned up at him. *No one thinks the FBI agent stole something at an overdone Christmas party,* she'd said to him. He'd winked and leaned closer to her. *But what if I did?*

You guys, I'd said, pretending to be annoyed by their affection. *Please.*

Shan is on a bad boy kick, Thomas had said with a smirk. *Just trying to please her.*

I'd pretended to gag.

Aunt Shannon died two days later. Our world spun upside down, and opening up my purse to be searched before I left

Westcotts' that night wasn't important anymore. I forgot all about the stolen ring.

"Oh yeah," is all I say to Mom.

She swallows, and I'm guessing my face played my emotions as I remembered. "Anyway, they haven't found it," she goes on. "I guess it's supposed to be Vivi's engagement ring, and she's getting married at Christmas. I understand it's upsetting, but Alexandra's being obnoxious about it. Every post she makes sounds like she's accusing everyone in the neighborhood of a conspiracy."

That seems like Mrs. Westcott. A couple summers ago, her dog got sick, and she called the police, insisting that some boys down the street had fed the dog beer.

"Why don't they just have a new one made?" I ask. It's weird that Mrs. Westcott wouldn't parade around the fact that they have plenty of money to replace something like that. "They probably even had insurance on it, right?"

"It's a family heirloom. Her husband's great-grandmother's. Westcotts have worn it for generations," she says the last in a posh voice that makes me laugh. She sobers. "I absolutely understand why she's upset. I should be more sympathetic." She grimaces, but she's struggling to hold it. "Anyway, what are you up to?" she asks.

"Work is slow until training camp starts. And I've been spending too much time at my apartment by myself. Re-reading TOK."

Mom chuckles. "Any special reason?"

Heat blooms in my cheeks immediately. "I actually met another fan, and you won't believe who it is."

Her eyes widen, and she leans in closer. "It's a guy, and you like him. I can tell."

I throw up my hands exaggeratedly. "Who wouldn't? He's hot, has a good job, and loves my favorite book series of all time."

"Well, who is he?"

"Brock Hunter. He plays for the Denver Devils." I tilt my head and give my mom a dreamy look that makes us both laugh. Like with Aunt Shannon, I've never shied away from dishing to my mom about all the details, even early on. We've always been close, and though we fought when I was a teenager, she was still my best friend no matter what. Sometimes she would call me her and Aunt Shannon's third musketeer. From the time I was little, they took me almost everywhere with them. Rarely was there a girls' night or trip that I wasn't invited to.

"Poor guy," my dad says, jogging lightly down the stairs.

"Steven!" Mom chides, amused.

Dad gives her a *what?* look. "Worst in the league two years in a row. Everyone's blaming players, but I say it's the coaching." He points a finger at my mom and moves to the sink to get a glass of water.

My dad is a former pro-football player. He played fifteen years as a defensive lineman for the LA Rays and was the biggest reason I got a position on the athletic training staff with them a couple years after I graduated from PT school.

"Better watch your mouth." Mom shakes her head at him, "unless you're going to start picking up calls from the general managers who want you on staff."

Dad grunts. "I'm retired."

Mom rolls her eyes, but she's smiling, and turns back to me. "Tell me about Brock Hunter and these books." Dad leans against the kitchen counter, listening in while he slowly drinks his water. I'm close to my dad too. Mom's best friend and a daddy's girl all at once. I rarely missed any of his home football games as a little girl and went to as many away games as Mom would let me. He injured his knee when I was ten, and he let me help him do the rehab exercises at home with him, which was when I fell in love with helping people through exercise. Thanks to Dad, I've always loved sports, so it seemed a given to use my physical therapy license on an athletic training staff somewhere.

Aunt Shannon thought going into regular practice was too boring for me anyway.

But talking to Dad about the newest boy I like? Embarrassing. Even at twenty-nine, it makes me squirm. I push the thoughts away because Mom will tell him anyway. She tells him everything. I just don't need to witness it.

"I met him at Lincoln's wedding."

"Ahh, that's right. They played at USC together," Dad interrupts.

I whip my head around to look at him. "Do you know everything?"

"He's retired," Mom parrots, and we both laugh. Dad finally joins our chuckling.

"Anyway," I go on, "he saw the TOK necklace that Aunt Shannon gave me and asked about it. One thing led to another and—"

Dad coughs. "That's my cue." He moves to leave the kitchen, setting down his glass inside the sink.

"*And we ended up talking about Obsidian Kingdom, Dad!*" I hurriedly cry out. I turn back to my mom. "We've just been texting. *Honestly.*" My cheeks burn so hot I could start a fire.

Dad continues out of the room. He turns to throw me a wink before heading into the family room. A moment later the TV comes on, already tuned to a sports broadcasting station and a group of people talking about the upcoming training camps.

I fan my face, hoping the blush is fading. I do wish that my night with Brock had included some romantic moments, but getting caught up in talking about TOK felt pretty heady too. I'm trying to manage my expectations, make sure I'm not falling too fast for someone I just met, but that's hard when he can analyze the tropes in Kael and Lyra's relationships with me. And especially when that someone is as good-looking as Brock. Plus we're texting all the time and getting to know each other like if we were going on dates.

"I have a crush on him," I say in my cool-as-a-cucumber

voice, which contradicts everything I'm saying. "I don't think it's any more than that."

"Yet." Mom wiggles her eyebrows.

I let out a long sigh. "I hope so."

Mom leans back in the upholstered chair she's sitting in. Her kitchen chairs are so fancy. She says it's because I'm finally out of the house and she can have nice things.

"It must be something," she says. "Shan basically set you up with him." She nods at my necklace, which I've been wearing every day since I met Brock.

"Yeah," I say in a soft voice, reaching up to hold it.

Mom looks just like her sister. She was older than Aunt Shannon by two years, but they were super close. Most people mistook them for twins. They had the same chestnut brown hair and gray-blue eyes, which I inherited from them. I have my dad's full lips and thick, unruly eyebrows, which require a lot of upkeep.

But sometimes, looking at Mom is like looking at Aunt Shannon, and it makes my breath catch. I wonder if it's ever hard for her to look in the mirror and see her sister in the reflection. I know she misses her with the same ache I do. Their closeness is the reason *I* was close to Aunt Shannon. She was like my second mom. When Mom married Dad twenty-five years ago and moved out to LA with him, Aunt Shannon followed from Arizona, where they'd grown up. They lost their parents when I was little, so sometimes Aunt Shannon even took on the role of grandma to me, making sure someone spoiled me and teased Mom when she protested.

"I opened my box," I say after the silence has stretched on too long.

Mom reaches out and takes my hand again, holding it in hers. "What was in it?" She wears a soft smile.

"Did she write you letters?" I ask. Mom nods, the smile growing, and I lean my elbows on the table, continuing. "When did she tell you to open them?"

Mom tilts her head in thought. "The first one is for the anniversary of her death. Then there's one for when you get married. When I get to be a grandma. My sixtieth birthday. One for if Steven dies first. I think that's it. What about yours?" Her eyes shine, but Mom likes to talk about Aunt Shannon, even when it makes her emotional. It helps her hang on to her sister, hearing the stories.

I tell her all the labels on mine, and like me, she catches her breath when I mention she wrote one for me for when Mom dies.

"Probably thought she was going to be here for you," Mom says with a hiccupping laugh. "We were only two years apart! I could have outlived her." She huffs. I lean out of my chair toward Mom, enveloping her in a hug.

I think of what Thomas texted me earlier. "She wrote them for Dad and Thomas too?" I ask.

"Yeah. Steven's are like mine, although she did write him a letter for when you meet the guy he knows is the one. And one when he's a grandpa, and if I die first."

"And Thomas's?"

"I only know about one, and only because she told me about it. I don't think Thomas has looked at them." She taps her fingers absently on the table. "When he meets someone new and it's real." Then she laughs.

"What?"

"She didn't want him to move on." Mom's teasing expression is a shade sad, her eyes dancing. "I mean, she did, but in the moment it made her crazy. She said she wrote up a whole letter about how she wanted him to love just her his whole life and then tore it up." We share a look with each other about how feisty Aunt Shannon was.

"I couldn't go through everything," I say because what I want to say is how unfair it is that Aunt Shannon was robbed of half her life, even more so than the five to ten years of life she should've had after her diagnosis. We were all supposed to have plenty of time to say goodbye, but in the end, her accident took her far too quickly.

Mom hums in understanding but doesn't talk. Probably taking a minute to settle her emotions back down.

"Well," she says after a moment, "what do we know about Brock Hunter?"

I let out a breath, glad she changed the subject. "He plays left-tackle for the Denver Devils. You've probably seen a few memes of him. His temper gets played up." I open my phone to show Mom the helmet one. Dad turns down the TV in the family room, scoffing as he tunes into our conversation. My mom has loved the open concept layout of the kitchen and family room of their house for this exact reason. When she was in the kitchen getting dinner ready, she didn't want to be cut off from whatever Dad and I were doing. I have memories of a lot of conversations where the three of us were split between these two rooms—the four of us when Aunt Shannon was around, which was a lot.

"I met him a few years back at a big pro-football charity event. What was it again?" He looks to my mom to help him remember, but she shrugs.

"You've done a million of those," she says.

"Hmmm." He frowns as he ponders. "I think we were putting together packages of some kind. Anyway, he worked harder than anyone and never complained." He chuckles to himself. "I remember he did call out some guys that weren't helping out, a couple rookies, you know? But from what I saw? Good guy. I'd play with him any day." He holds up a finger. "And Trent Foster, the Pumas' strength and conditioning coach, has only good things to say about him."

"Pumas?" Mom says.

"He signed with them after college," I explain.

"Undrafted!" Dad pipes up, in his impressed voice. I'm not surprised he admires the hard work Brock had to put in to play pro football. "Got traded for some linebacker the Pumas wanted a few years ago."

"Unfortunate for Brock," I say with a sigh. "The Devils don't seem to know what they've got."

"The Devils don't know a lot of things," Dad says.

"But the fact that he likes TOK seals the deal, am I right?" Mom bounces her eyebrows at me. Dad gives us a look and turns the volume back up on the TV, now that we've switched to talking about my crush again.

"Can you blame me?" I ask. He's fun, sending me quotes from the books and off-the-wall opinions he knows will get a rise out of me. He's a tease, even though it's dry. In his texts, I've seen bits and pieces of the intensity that people play up, but he's so much more.

Having a friend like him feels like the first few chapters of The Obsidian Kingdom when I read it the first time: fascinating, intriguing … engrossing.

From the text I got this morning, Brock is probably almost done with book two already—we both had to slow down a little the last few days after spending an entire day reading book one. I've been listening to the audiobook because I still can't find my old copy. It must be at my apartment somewhere, but not knowing sends a little buzz through my stomach when I think about it being missing. Aunt Shannon didn't buy me that copy, just book one of that old collection, but they're still all tied together. Reading my original collection has become like a tribute to her.

I push away from the table.

"Okay, I have to go. But have you seen my copy of Shattered Void?" I ask, just in case. "It's the second TOK book."

"Yeah," Mom says. "Your dad's been reading it. He borrowed it from your house a couple weeks ago. He didn't think you'd miss that old copy." She grimaces. "You have a couple other sets, right?"

I don't care that Dad borrowed a book from me without mentioning it. We've always been like that as a family, sharing easily. He probably meant to let me know and forgot.

"Dad is reading TOK?" I give my mom a bewildered look.

"I'm retired!" Dad says from the family room.

I burst into laughter. Dad has been retired from pro football for almost ten years. In the first several years after he retired, he always had something going on to keep him busy—commentating gigs and stuff like that, but in the last couple years he's stepped back from almost everything to be "totally retired" as he likes to tell me and Mom. Now he's free to golf. Fly out to Rays games across the country whenever he wants. Spoil grandkids when they finally arrive. (His pointed words, not mine.)

I move from the kitchen to the edge of the family room. "What do you think of the book?" I ask Dad, almost giddy. First, finding out that Brock likes the books, and now maybe my dad likes them too? I mean, he read on to book two. That means something. I form a picture of the two of them discussing the ultimate battle scene from book fifteen, but quickly dismiss it. Managing expectations.

Dad smirks at me. "Meh." But his eyes dance.

"Dad!" I turn on my heel and wave as I head back the way I came, bending over to kiss Mom on the cheek before I leave, grinning the whole way. "Want to be in my book club with Brock Hunter?" I call from the doorway before I go.

"Meh!" he answers again, a wide smile breaking his face.

September & October

Presley: FINALLY finished Whispers of the Forgotten Empire. I do not remember that one being so long. Seven hundred pages!? What was Thornridge thinking?

Brock: You're on book 7 already?

Brock: That's it. I'm quitting football.

Presley: 😂 What, like you're busy? You act like you have to practice or play games or go to a job or something.

Brock: You guys played New York last week. That's at least eight hours of reading time just on the plane. Cheating.

Presley: 😂 You guys were in Florida! Just as long of a flight.

Brock: I was sleeping. I was a little bit tired. 🫥

Presley: Sorry I didn't watch. We were playing the same time. How did it go?

Brock: 😑 Same as always.

Presley: <hug gif>

Presley: Greatness isn't forged in comfort and ease but when you stand on the edge of despair.

Brock: Did you just quote Lyra to me?

Presley: Name that book.

Brock: Psh. Easy.

…

…

Presley: You don't know, do you? 😂

…

Presley: I know you're cheating and searching. If you didn't have the set in ebook, you wouldn't be a true fan.

Brock: Eternal Wrath of the Void

Presley: smh

Presley: Are you still on book 5 <laughing emoji>

Brock: No comment.

Brock: That's what I've been instructed to say.

Presley: You can say anything to me, football or TOK or whatever.

Brock: I know.
Presley: So.
Presley: What do you *want* to say?
...
Brock: This team is never going to be a team until we decide that Thompson is a qb worth putting it on the line for. That we have eight all-stars on this team and can't win a game.
Presley: My dad says the coach needs to be fired.
Brock: No comment.

————

Presley: You have a new meme! I told Eli it was better than his touchdown celebration dance meme. He disagreed. 😂 <GIF of Eli Dash's celebration dance>
Presley: <Meme of Brock Hunter standing on the sidelines, arms folded, ignoring the player next to him>
Presley: "When your favorite fantasy book series author is holding hostage the long-awaited book sixteen."
Brock: 🤦
Presley: 😔 Is it too soon? 😬
Brock: No. That face palm was because of your bad joke. You can't come up with anything better. Like "When you find out Lyra is the Obsidian Queen."
Presley: "When your bestie keeps trying to ruin your life"
Brock: "When your bestie can't face reality and you're going to have to be the one dealing with her tears."
Presley: 🙄
Presley: When the defense only rushes three guys and the quarterback still only has half a second to throw and only one offensive lineman bothers to stay in to save the qb from ending up under a pile of defenders.
Brock: That's what Lincoln said.
Presley: He's stealing my jokes!

Brock: 😂 He wasn't smart enough to send the meme, if it makes you feel better. Just the basic sentiment.

Presley: How are people making this a thing? They're so dumb.

Presley: You didn't even throw a water cooler this time.

Presley: I could take pictures of half our team looking exactly like that on the sidelines. 🙄

Brock: Can't believe I'm the one saying this, but you gotta ignore social media.

Presley: I can NOT ignore people who believe anything they see on the internet.

Brock: What story is it this time? The one about how my dad made me do pushups all the time and that's why I am the way I am.

Brock: Impressive for a guy that never saw me play.

Presley: I refuse to repeat this nonsense.

Presley: However, me and the boys ride at dawn.

Brock: You and the boys?

Presley: Me and my posse. They're quite large football players. These people will regret their actions.

Brock: This is the third time this year I've been a meme. Are you going to be like this every time?

Presley: Probably.

Presley: I'm setting people straight.

Brock: Presley. Stop poking the trolls. It only makes them worse.

Brock: <GIF of basketball player pulling another player back>

Brock: Why are you scrolling X right now?

Presley: How did you know it was X?

Presley: New York is beating the Cobras 63 to 14. My dad is holding me hostage. I'm bored.

Brock: It's always X.

Brock: Don't you have book nine to finish?

Presley: I needed a break.

Brock: I don't want your pity breaks.

Presley: I got to the scene where Finn kisses Lyra.

Presley: So I needed a break. 😩

Brock: 😆 And X was the better choice?
Presley: Really tells you something, doesn't it?
Brock: You do remember that Lyra ends up stabbing Finn in the shoulder a couple chapters later, right?
Presley: I DESPISE that she kisses back.
Presley: gag gag gag
Brock: <screenshot of fan art of the Lyra-Finn kiss>
Presley: I take it back.
Presley: You're no longer my bestie.

Presley: We're going to be in the same city next week.
Presley: For the first time since June!
Presley: A Brock and Presley Book Club reunion. It's going to be epic.
Brock: 😆 TBH I'm trying to temper my expectations for my weekend in LA.
Presley: I wish I could reassure you in some way, but you are coming to play my team and I know we're going to win.
Brock: You're still mad about the fan art picture I sent, aren't you.
Presley: I've forgiven you, Brock Hunter. Doesn't mean I've forgotten.
Presley: I wish you had time for dinner. It would be so fun to hang out. I found this quirky tavern-style restaurant in East Hollywood that's exactly what I imagine the Broken Crown looks like.
Presley: I'm sure you're hurrying back to spend Thanksgiving with your mom.
Brock: Kurtis surprised her with a ski trip to Breckenridge since I was going to be out of town and couldn't get back to Denver until late.
Brock: I'm doing Thanksgiving dinner with Lincoln and Layla.
Presley: Jealous. I've heard that dinner's going to be bussin.

Brock: Yeah, especially for me after I lose to those guys. 😂

Presley: With Mila coming, I bet the pie will be worth it.

Brock: The only reason I'm going.

Brock: You should come too. You know they would all love it.

Presley: Are you explaining to my mom why I'm ditching her to celebrate a holiday with the guys I work with all the time?

Brock: You say that in a way that makes it seem like I should be afraid of her when we both know how nice she is.

Presley: It's the nice ones you have to worry about.

Presley: But text me if you want to hang out after.

Brock: I'm starting to question why all my friends are associated with the Rays.

Presley: It really says something about you.

CHAPTER 6

BROCK

Thanksgiving

I wouldn't have picked up the phone for anyone after that loss, not even my mom or Tim. But something about talking to Presley appealed to me. Knowing she'll tell me silly jokes and then be serious with her comfort and then tell me another silly joke to lighten the mood makes her the perfect person to talk to right now. So when the phone rings with a Facetime call as I take a LetsRide over to Lincoln's for Thanksgiving dinner, and it's Presley's face on the caller ID, I press the green button.

"Happy Thanksgiving!" she says as soon as I pick up. She's grinning, but the hesitancy in her eyes proves she didn't think I was going to answer. I smile at the thought of her taking a chance.

"If you're here to tell me that you finished book ten this afternoon, our friendship is over," I tease.

Her shoulders jump with a quick laugh. "Maybe if I hadn't been at a football game, doing my job."

I grimace and think about the hit the Rays quarterback took early in the fourth. They were winning by three touchdowns by that point, so he didn't come back in. Didn't stop speculation that he was seriously hurt.

She waves her hand, confirming my theory. "He's totally fine. Just being cautious. He'll have a nasty bruise on his thigh tomorrow, but no worse for wear."

"That's good to hear."

"Wait," she says, leaning closer to the phone, her big brown eyes filling up the screen. "What are you wearing?"

Honestly, what I'm wearing is my best effort at cheerfulness today. I brought it to LA knowing we were probably going to lose to the Rays and I'd be eating dinner with a bunch of Rays players. I don't want their pity; I want to enjoy their company. So I'm showing up in a funny Christmas sweater with a picture of Rudolph in a football helmet, his antlers sticking inexplicably out of holes in the side.

I pull my phone away so she can get a good look, and she beams at me. "That's so good. Are there lights on his antlers?" she asks, leaning in again. "Like real lights?"

I press a button on the bottom of the shirt and they blink.

"Seriously. That's so awesome. I don't think I could top that."

"Just a second," I say to her as the LetsRide pulls up in front of Layla and Lincoln's house. I pay my driver and walk up the sidewalk, hovering midway so I can talk to Presley before going in.

She takes a deep breath. "Hey. How *are* you?" she asks, her tone softer now that she knows I'm alone. My sweater is forgotten in her concern for me.

I clench my jaw. "Feeling dumb." I knew she'd ask something like this. I knew I'd want to tell her, that I'd feel safe telling her. I think it's so easy to confide in her partly because of the distance between us and partly because our friendship revolves around a book series seventy-five percent of the time. Every confidence is safe.

"You were right."

"I shouldn't have said it out loud. Especially not in the press room." I run a hand through my hair and then pace a few steps back down the sidewalk. There's going to be a call from someone soon. The coach, the GM, my agent. I can feel it. Everything is tight in my chest. I haven't let my mouth run like that for years. I've kept my emotions under a lid, only ranting to people I trust, like Mom, Tim, and now Presley. And I can't say what it was about this game in particular that made me snap. Maybe it was nothing about this game. Maybe it's the fact that we've only won two games out of eleven so far this season, and no one seems to want to fix what *can* be fixed. So Thompson's throwing interceptions? He gets about three seconds, max, on passing plays to make something happen. He's as desperate as me. I'm doing my best to protect him, but I can't say the same for the rest of the line. And our receivers? Our all-star, Harris, acts like if Thompson doesn't throw him a dime on every pass, that if he has to step one toe out of his route, Thompson is the whole problem.

"Nobody's perfect," Presley says.

"Especially not me."

"'Falling into darkness does not define you. It's rising back up. Every scar tells a story, not of weakness, but of your strength to rise again.'"

Emotion catches in my throat. I swallow it down and force lightness to my reaction. "Do you have a TOK quote for every situation?"

She laughs, sounding forced. "There are fifteen books. Bound to be something that applies to pretty much everything. And…" She presses her lips together and holds up a small, hardbound notebook with a floral scene on the front. "It turns out my aunt liked TOK more than I realized. I think she read all of them, and she wrote down the quotes she liked in this notebook. I found it a few weeks ago." She clears her throat. "The box she left me?" she reminds me. We talked about it in our first phone conversation.

"This was in there the whole time. I thought it was going to be motivational quotes or something—well, I mean they are. I didn't realize they were going to be from TOK. Like they were just for me." Her voice is watery by the time she finishes. She shrugs, like this isn't a big deal.

"Or for me." I wiggle my eyebrows at her, trying to lighten the mood.

"But really, Brock. You expressed frustration that everyone on the team was feeling. Did you see Thompson next to you? He nodded when you said that part about how nothing is going to change in Denver until the all-stars start acting like it." Her expression is eager, wanting me to believe her that everything will be all right.

And something in my chest does loosen at the fact that she watched the press conference, that she noted how Thompson reacted so she could report some solidarity from the team for me. Pretty soon everyone will have seen the clip—another blow up from Brock Hunter? Guaranteed social media clicks. Especially since it's been a while.

"Thanks, Pres."

She holds up a paperback. "Also, I'm within fifty pages of finishing ten, sucker. Gonna happen tonight before my pie coma takes over."

I snort, and my shoulders fall down, tension draining. It's not a surprise that Presley can do this. Her quirky cheerfulness, the way she teases me without shame—she's been what I need during another tough season. "Enjoy this victory. It won't last."

She raises her eyebrows. "I can keep my book with me at the facility, reading between patients. Until I see a picture of you at practice with a book to read in between plays, I'm not worried."

I point a finger at her. "Careful what you wish for, Tatum."

She lets out an amused scoff about the same time Lincoln opens his front door, steps out onto his porch, and calls, "Are you coming in?"

"Just a minute." I wave him away. He notes that I'm on the phone and then goes back into his house, scooping up his daughter on the way in since she followed him out. Bells on a green Christmas wreath jingle as the door closes.

Presley's cheeks have turned red when I look back at her. "I forgot. You're doing dinner with Lincoln and Layla and their families. I'll let you go."

I don't want our conversation to be over, but she's right that I need to get inside. Especially because Lincoln's going to read into this more than there is. He, Eli, and his cousin-in-law, Landon, think that every good relationship starts off with a friendship and so, naturally, my relationship with Presley must be something more.

"Enjoy your turkey and pie," I say as a goodbye.

"You too." She waves and hangs up quickly.

Sighing, I shove my phone in my pocket and climb up the steps to the front door. Since Lincoln was just out here and they're expecting me, I tap on it and let myself in. The house smells like turkey and pie, and my stomach rumbles with anticipation. A big band version of "White Christmas" plays in the background. According to Lincoln, Layla starts with Christmas as soon as Halloween is over and Thanksgiving is just part of the Christmas season.

"Hey, Brock!" Layla greets me first as I walk into the decorated living room. As expected, the Christmas tree is up, sparking with blue and yellow lights, and all the ornaments football themed, which makes me grin. Layla sets down a bowl full of mashed potatoes on the long table in the dining area and then comes toward me, taking me by the shoulders to pull me down and kiss my cheek. "I'm so glad you could come," she says when she steps away. "Great sweater," she adds with a soft laugh.

"Thanks for having me."

Lincoln invited me before he knew that my mom's boyfriend, Kurtis, was taking her away for the weekend. Having the invitation helped Mom feel less guilty for going. She was so excited when she told me about Kurtis's surprise. She's texted twice since the game, offering to meet me in Denver with dinner tonight, and I've assured her Lincoln will take good care of me.

Lincoln comes in with Margot still on his hip and pulls me into a one-armed hug. "Nice," he says with a smirk at my sweater, and then adds, "Great game."

I scoff.

"No, seriously." He keeps a grip on me "*You* had a good game. You did everything you could." He pats my shoulder reassuringly before dropping his hand.

"Except keep my mouth shut."

Lincoln rolls his eyes. "Everyone's thinking it. So you said it out loud."

"That's what Presley said." Basically.

I can tell Lincoln likes the subject change by the way his smile spreads. "Oh, was that Presley on the phone?" He sounds so innocent, but he's just waiting to share his opinions.

I reach for Margot to see if the one-year-old will come to me. I don't see her often, and Lincoln says she's going through a phase where she only wants Layla and Lincoln and sometimes her grandparents.

Like I expected, she snuggles into Lincoln's side, and he kisses the top of her head. She does reach out to touch the still blinking lights of my sweater, small fingers brushing over them in curiosity before she pulls them back with a cautious look at me.

"No hard feelings," I assure her, holding out a fist toward her with one hand and using my other to gently lift her fist to bump it. At least I get a smile out of her.

"What did Presley have to say about it?" Lincoln asks too casually, heading into the kitchen and picking up some plates with his free hand. I follow as well and grab the silverware that's set out.

"We're just friends, Linc," I remind him.

He pauses at the table, eyeing me. "You found someone who's as obsessed with those books as you, is beautiful and successful, and who you like spending time with, and you're not interested in pursuing it romantically?" His voice holds a stadium full of skepticism.

I think I would know if Presley was The One, the way Lincoln knew pretty much right away with Layla. The way my mom is all starry-eyed over Kurtis. How Tim and Meg still orbit around each other even after all these years. Their feelings are so obvious.

"It's not like that. We're friends," I say. Lincoln puts down the plates and stares at me. "What?" I ask defensively. "Yeah, I like talking to her and spending time with her, but that's it."

He blinks at me and I shrug, a non-verbal repetition of *What?*

"So what exactly are you looking for in a romantic partner, B?" He resumes placing the plates around the table, and I follow him, setting out forks, spoons, and knives. "Someone who's hard to talk to and is kind of a pain to be around?"

I huff. "I don't know how else to say it. It's not like that with us."

Lincoln looks at Layla, who's putting turkey-printed napkins down on top of the plates. I like the laid-back vibe of this dinner. The settings are nice, but neither Lincoln nor Layla seem overly concerned about the setup. I'll be happy to relax, eat good food, and hang out with his family.

Once he stops grilling me about Presley.

He pauses, holding the last plate in his hand and scowling at me. "Natasha."

My cheeks immediately burn. "That was different."

Lincoln arches an eyebrow. "Because…?"

It's not fair that he's bringing up the one serious girlfriend I had in college. We were kids then, both full of ourselves to be starting at USC. "I was distracted. We had a lot going on, Linc. And I was young. It's not the same."

"Who's Natasha?" Layla asks.

"The girl Brock dated our junior and senior year. Well, once he finally opened his eyes. She spent four months bringing dinner over to our house and offering to help B with math and painting his number on her face for every game before he got it." He eyes me pointedly.

"Presley has never painted my number on her face." She's never been flirty with me, not even when she's being funny. It's always friendly teasing and ribbing, like with Lincoln or Jett. *Friendly*. Natasha was years ago.

Lincoln lays the last plate down, and then takes a step back. "Okay, bro. I'll take your word for it, but I guess just be careful."

I lay down the last set of silverware and scowl up at him. "Careful about what?"

"Other … people might be seeing what I'm seeing too. That's all." He turns and heads back into the kitchen. Margot wiggles in his arms, and he sets her down. She eyes me, then backs away, into the living room. I try not to appear too threatening, smiling and even taking a step away. But I'm not in denial about my large size. Bigger than her dad, for sure. Once she's safely parked in front of her basket of toys, I head into the kitchen.

"Other people meaning Presley?" I ask Lincoln. "You think I've led her on."

"No. Not that I know of. I'm just saying, it's easy to blur the lines, and you don't want anyone—"

"Presley," I say dryly.

"—getting the wrong idea."

"She doesn't have the wrong idea, because we've never flirted or anything. We mostly talk about books and some other life stuff, like friends do." I watch as Lincoln slices the turkey, and then I move to do the same to the beef brisket. "And in case you were wondering, I don't have feelings for you either. Just to clear the air."

Lincoln snorts. "Good to know. I'm taken, by the way." Layla laughs as she comes into the kitchen with us, wrapping her arms around him from behind.

I set the brisket I've finished slicing next to the turkey. "What else can I do to help?" I ask her.

She shakes her head. "We're done setting up. You can relax in the living room until everyone shows up. Maybe Margot will even come sit on your lap for a second."

"You don't have to ask me twice." I leave them to have a minute of alone time and head for the living room to coax Margot into playing with me. Maybe the lights on my shirt will win her over.

Within ten minutes, the house fills with people. Both Layla and Lincoln's parents show up, as well as Layla's cousin Landon and his wife, Mila, and Mila's brother, Eli Dash, and his wife Court. Her aunt comes as well. I met everyone at Lincoln's wedding, but I knew Eli before the wedding through football. It's a small world. We've never played on a team together, but there's still a camaraderie between players for the most part.

Besides some good-natured ribbing from Eli about the game, dinner is good and what I needed after a day like today. As usual, the combined Knight-Delaford-Dash clan treats me like I'm one of them. I'm as comfortable here as I would be at my mom's house or with Tim and his family.

I'm one of the last to leave, around eleven p.m. I order a Lets-Ride to come pick me up, but I don't want to go back to the hotel. Lincoln would let me stay here if I asked, but I've already overstayed my welcome. He probably wants some quiet time with his wife. It's been a full day.

Going back to my hotel means maybe running into teammates, some of whom aren't too happy with me. A lot of guys flew home right after the game to be back in Denver with their families, but more than a few stuck around too. Plus the hotel will be lonely. I'm not falling asleep any time soon. Not after what happened today at the press conference.

I could see if Presley wants to hang out. I haven't seen her in person since the wedding and a glimpse of her on the sidelines at the game today. I pull out my phone, and only hesitate because of what Lincoln said about not blurring the lines. I would never want to hurt Presley, but she doesn't see us like that either. Neither of us do.

I shake off Lincoln's evaluation of the situation. He has it all wrong.

Brock: You up?
Presley: Am I up whooping your butt getting through this book? Yes, yes, I am.
Brock: Wanna hang out?

CHAPTER 7
PRESLEY

"What happened here? Did someone break in?" Brock teases when I open the door.

He has a fair point. My tree is up but bare. A couple boxes sit at the foot of it and some decorations are pulled out and strewn around the tree. I was contemplating how to arrange everything when he texted. I've also dug around for my best ugly Christmas sweater, though it's no match for Brock's. It's green and has Santa's face on it, only Santa's face is my dad's face with a white beard and a jaunty red Santa hat. Mom and I got them last year to top our Christmas pajamas. But Brock's so adorable in his, and I don't know if I can get over it. It's like he's trying to make himself irresistible to me.

"It's Beginning to Look a Lot Like Christmas" is playing quietly from a speaker, and there's hot cocoa on the stove that I made while I waited for him to get here. (And okay, a few splatters around the pan. And on the counter. The floor. I was excited and in a hurry.)

I throw my arms around Brock's waist and hug him. This is only the second time I've seen him in real life, but we talk and text enough that he feels like a much closer friend. A hugging friend.

He confirms this when his arms come around me and he lifts me up a little into him. He smells like turkey and rolls with the slightest waft of a tangy deodorant, and I want to giggle.

"Thanks for letting me come hang out," he says into my hair.

I pull away just enough to look up at him. My heart is hammering from our hug, but I won't let him know that. "I'm glad you texted." I take his hand and pull him into the room before dropping it and shutting the door. "Now I can read aloud to you the kissing scene I just got to." I clap my hands together.

Brock's eyes widen, and I can't keep a straight face.

"Kidding! Kidding!" I grab his hand again and pull him toward the kitchen. "Want some hot cocoa?"

He chuckles. "Yeah, I'd love some." But he doesn't let go of my hand. He tugs me closer, squinting at my shirt with that pondering expression that used to make me think he was mad. "What's on your sweater?"

I hold out my sweater and display it. "My dad. As Santa."

He points at me, grinning wide, which was goal number one for tonight—cheer up Brock. "It doesn't have lights, but otherwise, that's legit, Pres."

"Thank you." I drop my sweater and move to the kitchen. I grab the mugs I set out and ladle some hot chocolate from the pot into each one. "I've got a couple basic syrups," I offer, holding out my hand toward where I've set them on the counter. "Caramel, butterscotch, vanilla. Plus creamer. And marshmallows."

"Butterscotch, for sure. And marshmallows." He takes the mug when I've offered it to him after adding the syrup and mini marshmallows. "You take your hot chocolate seriously."

I add caramel and creamer to mine. "Who doesn't?" I shrug and then grin at him. I can't help it. I'm so excited to have him here. This is way better than staying up late to finish reading book ten and then texting Brock that I've beaten him. Again.

"To be honest," I say, leading him back to my living room. "I'm serious about Christmas. And once the turkey dinner is over, Christmas spirit explodes in my house. Okay, actually before Thanksgiving, because I'm the boss of myself, and if I want to celebrate Christmas before, I can." I'm rambling, so I clamp my lips shut and take a mental deep breath. My feelings for Brock will be obvious if I keep up like this, and although we're friends, I can't tell if he'd be interested in more yet. "What do you want to do?" I ask, hoping my voice sounds calmer and not like a crazy Christmas elf. "I can't offer typical Christmassy things like sledding or beautiful walks while the snow falls. This is LA. But we can watch a Christmas movie or play my Christmas version of 'Obsidian Kingdom: The Board Game.'"

He laughs, his shoulders shaking, and I love the visual. Maybe because I know what a hard day today was for him. Being apart from family on a holiday, thanks to a job, is never fun. Having that job suck is even worse, and then imagine having to talk to reporters afterward. One big barrel of ick.

"There's a Christmas version of the TOK board game?" he asks.

It's a fair question. The fact that there's a board game at all belies how very small the fan base is. Small, but fiercely loyal. So yes, there's a board game and there's a Christmas version of it, and there's a fan out there who's made a hundred dollars in their Etsy shop on it, mostly from me, I'd guess.

"Of course there is." I give him a look of faux innocence. "You don't have it?"

"Not the Christmas version."

I'm the one who bursts into laughter now. "But you have the regular one!" It's not a question, but an exclamation of triumph. I'm so dangerously close to falling in love with this man, and that's not normal to do because someone obsesses over the same books as you. I promise, it's more than the books. It's the fun we have texting and talking. It's the kindness I see in him that the world doesn't get a peek at. Not many see that when you're talking about a pro-football player who's larger than life and has all his worst moments blown up on social media. And that sweater. This huge guy in a funny sweater on a bad day.

"My mom was trying to connect with me as a teenager. I've heard I was kind of difficult."

"You? No way." I pretend shock.

He shakes his head. "Do you have the regular version of the board game too?"

"Yeah," I say, my tone conveying *of course.*

"What's the difference?"

"The Christmas version is red and green. It also comes with a Christmas tree centerpiece."

He studies me for several seconds, squinting at me in amusement. I am totally winning at cheering up Brock. Yeah, I watched his press conference. It was on the TV in the facility while I looked at a couple guys who got banged up—not Eli Dash. My boss was taking care of him. There was so much frustration in Brock's tone in every answer he snapped at the reporters until he broke and let everything spill out.

And the truth is I caught a few of our guys murmuring agreement with what he said.

"And you have both because…?" Brock asks.

"Because *Christmas.*"

He looks down at his cocoa. "Right. Christmas."

I set my cocoa on the side table next to my end of the couch. "So, board game, Christmas movie, or if you have another idea, I'm open." It's so hard not to just grin my face off that he's here, but I try to stay chill as I lean back against the squishy cushion of my couch.

Brock takes another slow sip and then lets out a long breath. Hot cocoa is magic like that. "What kind of Christmas movie are we talking? Like Hallmark…" He lets the sentence dangle, and even though he's not saying how he feels about that, it's all over the cringe he can't quite keep off his face.

"Whatever you want. I love Christmas movies of many

genres. Between streaming and rentals, the Christmas movie world is in the palm of your hands."

"You're letting me choose out of pity, right?" He narrows his eyes at me.

Of course I am. His team lost 31-7 on Thanksgiving Day. "Are you mad about that?" I pick up the remote from the side-table and turn on the TV.

He sets his cocoa down on the matching side-table on his end and settles back against the couch. "Not at all. How about *White Christmas*?" I can't hold back my surprise, and he says, "What?"

"Honestly, I was expecting you to be *A Christmas Story* or *Diehard* type of guy." I start searching for a place to stream the movie.

He chuckles. "I actually hate *A Christmas Story*. Like intense levels of loathing."

I gasp. Brock and I are actual soulmates. Well, in a friend kind of way. (For now, a little voice says, and I ignore it.) "Me too!"

"Is that pity agreement? Everyone loves that movie." Then he shudders and closes his eyes for a second.

I'm giggling. I can't help it. "I promise. It's the worst. That leg lamp. I don't know what it is. I can't get over it."

"I *know*! It's so weird."

"You should have known I didn't like it," I say as I click around to rent *White Christmas*. "TOK lovers are a rare breed. It makes sense that we'd all share similar tastes in a lot of things."

"There's a user on the website forum who named all of their children after the commanders of the Forces of Vorath and claims that Lord Vorath had some good ideas, politically, you know." Brock says this with a completely straight face, though his lips twitch with amusement.

I turn and blink at him. "That has to be a joke."

His eyes dance. "In any case, I was relieved to find out shortly after I met you that you didn't have any children who could be named after representatives of the Eternal Darkness."

I snort. "Obviously my children will be named Lyra and Kael."

"That's fair."

The movie starts and we settle in to watch. I'm grateful that Brock has no problem chatting during the movie, commenting on his favorite parts. I can rarely keep my mouth shut during movies, especially if I've seen it a few times. We fit together so perfectly. I force myself not to say anything weird like that. Telling him that *we'd both like a movie* is enough cringe for one night.

When he shifts into a more comfortable position—legs up on the large ottoman in front of the couch, head leaned against the back of the couch, and arms snuggled in a small, knitted blanket —I know he's going to fall asleep. It's been a long day, and I suspect the reason why he didn't want to go back to the hotel yet, but it's still past midnight and he's probably been up since five or six this morning.

Within a few minutes, his eyes close. I swallow back amuse-ment at the way he snaps them open before they drift shut again. It's exactly what my dad does when he's fighting to stay awake during a movie.

I stand up, and Brock's gaze shoots to me. "Bathroom break," I whisper, pointing down the hall. "Be right back." I know what I'll find when I come back, and that's the point. Without me in the room, he won't feel bad about giving in to closing his eyes —*just for a minute.*

Sure enough, by the time I return, he's breathing deeply. I settle onto my side of the couch and watch him shamelessly. The night we met at Lincoln's wedding has existed in a bubble for me. Fun, one of the best nights of my life, and it was so comfortable sitting and chatting with him about my favorite characters, the settings, the crazy plot twists, and the magical moments of that series. We talked about our lives and our families between that. But it was all surreal, this tall, muscled, gorgeous football player with a killer smile and soft eyes, hanging out at a table off to the side of the dance floor with *me.*

Don't get me wrong, it's not the whole football player thing. I'm around them all the time, famous ones, too, like Eli Dash, Mark Travis, Anthony Hurley, and Lincoln Knight. They're real guys who aren't that much different from the rest of us, but that doesn't change the fact that it was special that Brock chose me to talk to because he's … Brock. Lincoln Knight is still his best friend, even though they haven't played on the same team together for years. Given what he's told me about playing for the Devils (and all the rumors), it's not surprising he doesn't have a close friend on his team. But I can tell that he's not the type of guy who's friends with everyone. He chooses carefully. And the night of the wedding, he chose me. We could have chatted about the books for a little bit and then he could have gone to dance with one of the actresses. Or hung out with the people he knew better, like the Rays players and their families.

But he stayed with me, and until he texted tonight, asking to come over, it was like a dream I'd had one time that was so good I'd made it into a memory.

Tonight he's real and sleeping on my couch. It's an honor that he felt safe enough here for that. I roll my eyes at myself for thinking it, but I can't dismiss the thought outright.

My crush on him is turning into so much more than a crush.

I'm actually falling for him, Aunt Shan, I picture myself saying to her.

Do it, she'd say back. *Go for it. What's the worst that could happen? A broken heart?* She'd wave her hand with that unimpressed eye roll. *You've been there, done that, and absolutely survived.* Especially in the months after her diagnosis, Aunt Shannon's advice took on a "live it up" vibe, but in a deep, meaningful way.

"*The only chains that hold you are the ones you use to bind yourself,*" she might have quoted from TOK book ten, the one I just finished—if she hadn't been keeping that huge secret that she'd read them all. I marked that quote in the notebook a couple days ago to share with Brock sometime.

I'm not scared, I tell her.

CHAPTER 8

BROCK

"Hey … Brock?"

A soft voice pulls me slowly from sleep, and I blink awake to find Presley leaning over me. She's put her long, chestnut brown hair into a bun on top of her head, and her brown eyes look bright.

"Pres?"

She crouches down next to the couch. "I wanted to let you sleep, but the PT in me thought it might not be great for your back. Also I figured you probably have an early flight in the morning you won't want to miss."

My chest warms at her thoughtfulness. This whole night, from the moment she called to check in on me and then when she welcomed me into her home, she's been taking care of me. I'm lucky I can call her a friend.

I also have a whole list of things to point out to Lincoln to prove that our relationship is purely platonic. Like how Presley sat on the opposite end of the couch from me and didn't try to make any moves or even flirt.

I stretch my arms over my head and then sit up, pulling my feet off the ottoman. "Thanks. I appreciate you looking out for me."

She beams. "That's what friends are for."

Friends. Exactly.

I slowly extricate myself from her couch and stand up, checking the time on my watch. Just after one a.m. I pull out my phone to get a LetsRide, but as soon as I open the app, Presley puts her hand over my phone.

"Let me drive you. It will be way easier." She grabs a hoodie from the back of the couch where she was sitting and laughs when I scowl at the Rays logo on it. "Sorry to tell you, I only own Rays hoodies," she says apologetically.

"You don't need to drive me," I say. She's already moving to the door, slipping her feet into a pair of sandals. "It's late."

"I don't have to work tomorrow. It's no problem. You'd have to wait forever for a LetsRide anyway." She motions for me to follow her. "Come on. Stop whining."

I put my hands up in surrender. I know that look. I'm going to lose this argument like I did when I tried to convince her that book six is basically a retelling of the Greek myth of Hades and Persephone.

We're both quiet on the drive. I'm exhausted, and the short nap I got on Presley's couch has only enhanced it. It's not just physical exhaustion either. My time with Lincoln and his family and then with Presley has been a good distraction, but I haven't been able to completely let go of the worry about what's going to come down from the Devils' general management after what I said today. Presley might be right that a lot of people are thinking it and that some of my teammates might agree. That doesn't mean anyone high up at the Devils will like what I did. I'm drawing attention to the failures in Devils management, which they're obviously trying to cover up.

When Presley pulls up to the hotel, I lean over to hug her. Lincoln would totally read into it if he knew how much I liked hugging her, and he wouldn't believe me that it's nothing beyond the comfort of someone who understands me so easily. Friends like that are hard to come by. I don't have anyone in

Denver I can trust like this. I'm friendly with some teammates, but I could never confide in them.

"Thanks for everything today, Pres." I squeeze her tighter and then finally pull away. She still has to drive home.

Her hands slide down my arms before she sits back, and I open the door with one hand. Goosebumps rise up along my arms, probably from air that rushed into the car. It's not cold in LA by any stretch of the word, especially for a big Wyoming boy. But my sweater is lightweight and the blast of air is a surprise.

"Anytime," she says.

I reluctantly step out of the car, wishing I could hang out another day or so with Presley, but my flight is already set, and I have practice on Monday, bright and early.

Who knows, maybe by Monday I'll have all the free time in the world. My chest tightens at the thought, bringing back all the worries I was able to shed for the few hours I was with friends. I wave to Presley as I walk toward the hotel and she waves back. Then I hear, "I'm totally beating you to the end of book ten!"

When I turn around laughing, she waves vigorously out the window and then drives off. One good thing may come of me getting fired: I could beat Presley to the end of book fifteen for sure.

———

WE'RE EXPECTED to be at the facility early Monday morning since we lost. Even though I told Mom not to interrupt her vacation for me, she'd insisted on coming to Denver on Friday anyway. She and Kurtis even picked me up from the airport. Hanging out with them was a good distraction from worrying, but now that I'm at practice, that ball of anxiety I battled all weekend returns in full force.

Our weightlifting workout first thing in the morning keeps my mind off things, but by the time I'm in meetings at mid-morning, there's nothing to do but think about what happened. I try to focus on the team meeting and the position group meeting that follows, but I feel like I've gotten the bare minimum out of what we're talking about. Pretty hypocritical considering my criticism on Thursday afternoon.

That's the thing. I should feel some loyalty and partnership with the guys in my position group, but I don't. Maybe we're all checked out because of what I did. They have every right to be mad about what I said. Attitudes aside, we're all here doing our best, even if we have different ideas of what the best thing to do is.

By the time we get to the field for the correction period, I'm holding myself back from doing everything full tilt. We're not wearing pads, just jerseys and helmets, so letting loose will get someone hurt, and that's the last thing I need to add to this mess. When we get to conditioning, I'm able to burn off a little steam.

That doesn't mean I head into the locker room calm, especially not when one of the assistant coaches comes to get me after my shower. This *could* just be another talking to. It's been a long time since something like this has happened, and maybe I've earned some good will. Hey, my comments have been all anyone is talking about after our spectacular loss to the Rays, so maybe my distraction from the bigger problems and the way they use that to ignore the issues will get me a pass.

But in my gut, I know that's not what this is.

Especially when the general manager is sitting in the office with the coach when I arrive.

CHAPTER 9

PRESLEY

I've been antsy all day, even though it's nothing compared to how Brock must be feeling. But every sports commentator in the business is weighing in about Brock's future, and none of them are saying anything good.

Lincoln stops by the training room when I'm helping Eli stretch out the leg he bruised on Thursday. "Everything's going to be fine," Lincoln says, and it's embarrassing that my emotions must be written all over my face.

"Have you heard from Brock?" I ask. I've gone back and forth on whether I should just text him about it. Are we that close yet? It's hard to say. So much of our friendship is built around TOK, even though there's more to it than the books. But when we do have the deeper conversations, we both seem to revert to book talk when we want to lighten things up.

Lincoln grimaces. "I haven't. But no matter what happens, he'll land on his feet. Brock is one of the best left tackles in the league. If the Devils let him go, someone's going to sign him."

"But what about the way people talk about him—the commentators, social media? They make it seem like this is really bad." I can't help but worry about how the reputation that the Devils have fed to make him the scape goat will affect his career.

Left-tackles don't normally have this kind of spotlight, and the spotlight that Brock's unfairly gotten is hurting him now.

Lincoln lets out a scoff. "People who actually know what they're talking about can see through the hype. Someone will sign him, Pres."

Maybe being free of the Devils would be for the best. Brock deserves a team that appreciates him.

Lincoln's words do their job though and ease my worries. Brock has handled a lot in his life. He can handle this too.

I just hate that it has to be this way for him.

I wait as long as I possibly can before breaking down and texting Brock around ten p.m. That way, if he's already in bed, he can easily ignore my text if he doesn't want to talk about it.

Presley: I've been thinking about you all day. How are you?

He answers much quicker than I expected. The bubbles pop up instantly and then his text comes through.

Brock: Team-less for the moment.

I immediately switch over to my phone app. I'd do a Facetime call, but Brock might not want anyone to see him right now. I tap on his name to call him.

"Hey," he says.

"Hey." Tightness winds in my chest. Lincoln said everything would be fine, but that doesn't stop the ache I feel at Brock's dejected tone. "This sucks."

He laughs softly, surprising me. "No TOK quote?"

"I don't think 'This sucks,' is a phrase common in fantasy novels, to be honest."

"Maybe in book sixteen." Brock's voice has lightened a tiny bit, which unwinds some of the tension in me. He lets out a sigh. "In some ways, it's a relief."

I glare at my lap, wishing I could be there with Brock now.

"The Devils don't deserve you. There's another team out there right now, ready to snatch you up."

I hear another sigh from his end, this one with less frustration than the first. "My agent says a couple teams have called, so that's promising."

"Brock, that's more than promising." I pump my fist into the air in silent celebration. "You just got let go today. Of course everyone else is smarter than the Devils."

Brock chuckles, another reason for celebration. "I know I'm going to be fine," he says quietly.

"But?" There's something in his voice that tugs at my heart, a vulnerability he doesn't let out very often. I know a lot of Brock's story, how his dad left when he was young and how much he struggled because of it. How hard his mom worked to give him the best she could, to afford the equipment and the fees to play on competitive travel teams to get him where he is now. It's important he's told me these things, but they're also a part of Brock's story that a lot of people know.

"I'm tired of having to prove myself over and over again."

"I'm sorry." What else do I say? It's not fair. He's a great football player, but he had to work hard for his scholarship to USC, send out a lot of tapes, have his coach make a lot of calls just to get colleges to look at him. He wasn't drafted, and he had to try out to even make it on a pro team—the Pumas. "It sucks, Brock. It really does. It's not fair."

"That time I thought for sure you'd have some perseverance quote for me."

I head into my bedroom where my aunt's TOK quote book is sitting on my nightstand. I flip it open. "'You're surprisingly bad at not walking straight into traps.'" I read the first one I come across and then laugh. "Why did she write that one down?"

"It's one of the best things Brynna ever says." Brock's own laughter paints his words. "I think I have that highlighted in my copy."

"Well. Words to live by, I guess."

"You can always count on TOK," Brock says. "Even when you can't count on anything else."

His words hold more seriousness than they should, and my heart twists at how true that must be in his life. "Amen," I say.

———

I HAVEN'T HEARD anything from Brock by the end of the next day, and Lincoln didn't know anything either when he came in for his treatment with one of the other trainers this morning. There're a lot of details to work out to get Brock signed with another team, and I force myself to believe there have already been offers.

But I can't keep texting him like I'm his girlfriend, with a right to know all the details of his life.

Gah! Why am I not his girlfriend with the right to know?

I have a huge crush, and I have no idea how Brock feels about me. We talk all the time, and our conversations feel like more than just friendship to me. Doesn't his coming over to my house late on Thanksgiving mean something? He could have stayed at Lincoln's, but he didn't. Because the Devils lost to the Rays?

I'm a mess.

Thankfully, Mom calls me less than an hour after I get home from work so I don't have too long to spiral. I answer the Face-Time call as I hang up the last of my Christmas tree decorations. "Hey, Mom. What's up?"

She's laughing, and it takes her a few seconds to calm down enough to answer. "You will not believe …" She has to interrupt herself to laugh again. "What Alexandra Westcott is doing *right now*."

The last time my mom was this amused by Mrs. Westcott's antics was the time she went around the neighborhood measuring everyone's lawn with the ruler and then getting into an argument with the president of the HOA after a bunch of people, including my dad, called to complain about her.

I don't have to guess before Mom turns the phone around and shows me the view of the neighborhood from her front window. I can see Mrs. Westcott standing on the porch of the house across the street from Mom's, wearing a black pantsuit, the blazer trimmed in white, and her hair pulled into a sensible chignon. She's wearing white heels in contrast, and this whole picture is funny enough in and of itself that I wouldn't need Mom to tell me why she's waving her arms emphatically at the man at the front door to get a good laugh.

"She has been going house. To. House," Mom says, little bursts of laughter interrupting the last few words. "Insisting she has the right to search their property for the missing ring."

"What?" I burst out, the word shaking with laughter. "How? How does she have the right?"

"I'm not sure!" My laughter has fed Mom's, and her words are turning high pitched with her amusement. "I was laughing so hard when she came here, I had to go upstairs, and your dad is so mad I ditched him that he won't tell me. But something about the whole neighborhood being suspects since we were all at her party last year."

"It will be a miracle if anyone shows up this year," I point out.

"Sweetie, most of the neighborhood, including us, are going just to see what she does! Did you see her rant on Facebook yesterday about the police doing nothing to solve this crime? She was trying to rally people to defund LAPD over it. It's ludicrous."

I have to admit, finding out how the self-styled detective is going to use her party to root out the thief is a good reason to still go to her party. Also the food is usually top notch.

Mom flips me back around, and we talk about work for a few minutes before she says she has to go and ask her next-door neighbor what Mrs. Westcott said to her. She hangs up before I can beg her to stay on the phone to distract me.

I huff and grab the box of Aunt Shannon's things I never finished going through. *That* will distract me. I pull out all the stuff I've already looked at—the letters, the jewelry, and the trinkets. They're all sitting on top, so I set them carefully on my bed and start pulling out other things to examine.

I pick up a book-sized brown paper bag and carefully slide the book out of it. It's a collector's edition copy of TOK book fifteen, *Rebirth of Darkness*. I already have this one. It's one of the collection that has the cover art redone by a fan artist who's now become famous for her fantasy book covers. Story is that Thornridge saw something she'd posted online and insisted on doing all fifteen books with her art. Only fifty sets were printed, which makes them kind of rare. Are they rare when there aren't that many fans to begin with? Brock has this collector's edition too.

So much for distraction.

I open the front cover and gasp. This one is signed by Gideon Thornridge. *Miss Tatum, You have the most charming aunt. She tells me you're something of a fan. Thank you from the bottom of my heart, Gideon Thornridge.*

Aunt Shannon has left no explanation for how she came to meet Gideon Thornridge and never told me about it. I don't have any other signed copies. He's a hermit, or something. The only signing he ever did was before I got into the books. Someone online posted once that it was after the first book came out and someone brought him a copy of *Lord of the Rings* to sign, thinking he was somehow J.R.R. Tolkein. Thornridge was so offended— maybe on Tolkein's behalf—that he refused to do another signing after that. That might not be the real story, but the fact remains that as rare as the collector's edition is, signed books by Thornridge are even rarer. From what I can tell in the forum, about twenty-five people have signed copies.

And I'm holding one of them.

That's when I start sobbing. I want more than anything to

text Aunt Shannon in all caps WHERE DID YOU GET THIS?!? But I can't. Because she left this in a box with zero explanation. She'd been gathering things for a while when she died suddenly —a fatal fall, thanks to progressing muscle weakness from the disease. But it was all cut so short. Did she mean to leave a note explaining everything and she didn't get to it? It's another instance of feeling short-changed by her death, feeling like we should have had more time to say goodbye.

I lay face down on my bed, crying for a solid twenty minutes. Silver lining: *this* is a distraction from not hearing from Brock.

I can text him now about the book. It'll blow his mind.

I should actually Facetime him so he can see it.

Maybe *he* needs a distraction. I'm so antsy, and I'm not even the one with my future to worry about. I pick up my phone to call and then set it back down. I'm in no state to talk to Brock, especially if things are still up in the air for him. Thanks to the sobbing, my emotions are still on edge. I'll probably start crying again if I call Brock, and that's the last thing he needs—dealing with my tears when he may want to shed some of his own.

I put the book on my nightstand and continue looking through the box, wary of what it will unleash on me next. I find a few of Aunt Shannon's favorite books, which isn't surprising. A couple romcoms—she was a sucker for them—and a literary novel she made me read with her that I despised. None of them are signed.

At the bottom of the box is a black velvet ring case. My eyebrows shoot up. The other jewelry that Aunt Shannon left me were all random pieces she knew would mean something to me: the necklace I got her for Christmas one year, or earrings from a boyfriend who turned out to be the worst and she started wearing them as a joke. I laughed so hard when she wore them to meet one of my boyfriends once. (Funny story, he turned out to be the worst too. That's probably why she gave me the earrings.)

Something about this box though feels different, so I steel myself.

It still doesn't prepare me for what I see. I gasp, then squeal, then drop the velvet box and cover my mouth with both hands.

It's the Christmas ring Mom and I were talking about.

The stolen one.

CHAPTER 10
PRESLEY

There's no way it's the real one. Right? But why would my aunt have a replica of this famous, stolen ring. I've already looked up the picture on my phone to compare, and they look exactly the same.

But this can't be the real one.

Yeah, Aunt Shannon was at the party, but she couldn't have stolen it, right? She and Thomas had joked about it—but could there have been something more?

No.

No.

We were all searched when we left, so how is it possible she had it?

I stare at the ring for a very long time, trying to puzzle it out. I don't think it can be real, but how can I find out? I can turn the ring in, and they can laugh at me and say it's a fake. But what if it is real? How do I explain why I have it? I was also at that party.

How do I explain why Aunt Shannon had it? Maybe it was an accident that she ended up with it—like it got lost that night, not stolen. Yeah! She found it and … didn't turn it in.

I should text Thomas. He would know exactly what to do. I

grab my phone and tap on his picture, which is still listed under favorites. He and Shannon were so close to getting married, that he was already like family to me, the cool, fun uncle I didn't get to keep. I can't bear to bump him from this spot for someone else.

I start typing … and then delete the words. Then type again. Then wonder if this is something I should even be *texting* about. Should I call him?

So remember how you were joking about stealing that ring? I think Aunt Shannon might have actually done it…

I stop as I'm about to hit the call icon. Thomas is an FBI agent —a law enforcement official. Will he have to turn me in if I tell him? Would it get him in trouble if he doesn't? I definitely don't want to put him in that position.

So what do I do?

Mrs. Westcott is searching the neighborhood, convinced someone she knows stole it. I understand how badly she wants her daughter to have this ring when she gets married, but she's relentless. What will she say about Aunt Shannon if she finds out about this? What will she try to do to my parents or me to punish us for it?

I bury my face in my hands. I definitely can't turn this in until I have more information. Aunt Shannon is dead. She can't defend herself.

I put the ring back in the bottom of the box, which is probably not a safe place for it, but I don't want to put it anywhere else for now. It's been fine for almost a year in there.

I rub at my forehead. I need to talk to someone. Looking at the rest of the stuff Aunt Shannon left me has been a roller coaster of emotions. I shake out my hands. Brock has enough on his mind. I'll tell him about the signed copy later. Hopefully as a celebration and not to cheer him up. I put the box from Aunt Shannon back in my closet, since leaving it out next to my bed feels irresponsible now, and then grab my keys and the signed TOK book and head to my parents' house.

———

"Wow." Mom holds the book and nods in a way I'm sure she means to look impressed. She knows how important TOK is to me, but she never liked the books. (She read a couple at my urging.)

I snatch it from her. I don't mean to be like this, but my nerves are on edge, understandably, and I feel like I'm going to explode with the information that I'm pretty sure Aunt Shannon stole the Christmas ring. But I can't. I don't know what Mom would say if I told her, and maybe I'm worried she'll tell me to turn it in. Or insist on turning it in herself. I can't do that to Aunt Shannon. Not yet. Mrs. Westcott was literally here earlier trying to search their house. What if she comes back?

Maybe Mom can ask her to sweep it under the rug, so to say, as a favor if we give it back.

Maybe Mrs. Westcott will laugh in Mom's face and have us both arrested for being in possession of stolen property. I glance at the front window, where Mom showed me how she was marching up and down the street, insisting she could search people's houses. There's no way she'd let this go.

I keep my focus on the book. "Mom. This is a really big deal." I hold the book to my chest.

"I know, sweetie."

"There are like maybe twenty-five signed copies *in the world*." I plop down into a chair across from where she sits in their family room, wishing I could talk to her about the ring and not just the book. My frustration is coming out in my annoyance about her reaction to the book.

Dad is appropriately engrossed in book four of TOK, which I loaned to him, with my knowledge this time. It's taking him forever, so I'm glad he's not actually officially in my TOK book club with Brock.

"Right." Mom nods again solemnly.

"How did Aunt Shannon even get this? And why didn't she

tell me? Did she say anything to you?" I fire off questions too fast for Mom to answer. Maybe she'll somehow know I need answers about the ring, too, since I have all the same questions about it.

"She never said anything to me." Mom shrugs.

So I spin on Dad. "What are they saying about Brock? Have you heard anything?" I pace across the kitchen toward the family room. Finding the ring is a distraction from obsessing over Brock's career status, all right, just not the kind that's making me feel better.

Mom answers before Dad can. "Why don't you ask Brock? I'm sure he'd be happy to update you."

"It's not like that with us. We're friends."

"Sweetie. No one spends that much time talking to someone they're just friends with."

"I spend that much time talking to you," I point out. She rolls her eyes.

Dad lowers his reading glasses and looks over at me. "Jeff says the Cobras are definitely going to be interested, and he thinks the Rays will make an offer," he relays, speaking of a buddy of his who used to scout for the Rays.

My eyes widen. "The Rays?" That makes sense. One of the offensive linemen got hurt in a pre-season game. I can't remember if he played left-tackle, the same position as Brock. But even so, the Rays aren't strong there anyway, and in the last couple years, the coach has been building what he's calling his dream team. He wants a group of guys who aren't just all-stars. He wants guys who are good players who play well together as a team. The complete package. Brock would fit right into that, plus, thanks to his friendship with Lincoln, he's already got a rapport with guys on the offense. The Rays GM and coach would know that.

"Jeff's sure there's going to be a good offer?" I ask.

Dad's scoffs. "Everyone is sure, Pres. The Devils are stupid to let him go over this. Coach Bell is too prideful. Doesn't like that everyone's agreeing with Brock, so he has to let him go instead of take a good, hard look at his team and the rumors that are piling up."

"Then why are all the analysts saying how bad this is for Brock and talking about how nobody wants to deal with his temper?" I squeeze my hands together. I definitely trust my dad more than any of the talking heads on the sports networks, but everything in me feels like it's bouncing around with energy.

"Clicks and views, Pres."

I let out a long breath. "Okay."

"You need to tell Brock," Mom says.

I turn and blink at her. "Tell him what? That Jeff thinks the Rays are going to make an offer? That's not going to help anything. Besides, I'm sure he knows already."

"No. Tell him about your feelings. I've never seen you so excited about someone, and you obviously care about him. Why waste time?"

"I don't know how he feels about me." I look over at Dad, like he might have something to contribute, but he's already raised his book back up.

"Obviously he feels the same," Mom says. "He texted you at eleven o'clock at night to come and see you on Thanksgiving." She says this like it's all the evidence I need.

It works. "He had a bad day, and we're friends."

"Exactly. He had a bad day, and he turned to *you*."

"Technically, he went to Thanksgiving Dinner with Lincoln first."

Mom sticks a finger into the romcom book she was reading when I came over. She and Aunt Shannon shared their love of romcoms, and they constantly passed books back and forth. I wonder how many of her books she gave to Mom. Probably most of them.

"You can't stay in this friendship afraid of what will happen if you say something," she says. "Friendships like this don't last forever. One of you is going to meet someone and then what you have now is gone anyway." She picks the book up and waves it at me, like this is all the evidence I need.

"Are you giving me advice from a romance book?" Ironic, considering the quotes I keep spouting to Brock. I thought of one today for him, from book five when Elysande says, "The one with hope is always brighter than one without, even when that hope falls through."

"Who better to give advice than someone who researches love regularly?"

She has a point. She has a lot of good points, actually. I'm falling for Brock. Hard.

The only thing holding me back is fear that he doesn't feel the same way and knowing that if he doesn't, I'll lose something precious. That's hard to swallow, but also not a good reason to hold me back.

Part of me wants more time to figure this out, but I've known Brock since June. He could meet someone else any day, and everything we have will go up in smoke. He might still text me about TOK, but it won't be like it is now.

I stand up. "Well, I'm going home." I pick up the collector's edition and put it carefully inside my bag. I'm going to stop and buy a display case for it on the way home.

"There's leftover banana cream pie," Mom says. I don't know why she didn't lead with this when I walked in the door. Pie would have helped a lot of the nerves still pinging through me like tiny kickers are having punting practice in my stomach. I put my bag back down.

"Okay, I'll stay for a little pie."

Presley: YOU WILL NEVER BELIEVE WHAT I HAVE TO TELL YOU.

Brock: Please don't yell at me, Granny Presley. I don't have the bandwidth for it today.

Brock: And if this shouting is about you finishing book 10, save it. I finished it this morning and then listened to book 11 on 3x speed. Just got done. BOOM.

Presley: Okay, now who's the grandparent?

Brock:

Presley: I can't believe this. I'm so tempted to call that cheating and say it's not actually reading, but people who say that about audiobooks are trolls, so fine.

Presley: MY NEWS IS STILL BETTER AND WARRANTS SHOUTING.

Presley: Also I need to Facetime you. Can I? This needs to be SEEN.

Brock: How about I check it out in person? Just flew in for a meeting. Want to grab dinner?

CHAPTER 11
BROCK

Something I like about Presley is that she lets me be dramatic. When I sent her a text that I was in town, she didn't demand answers right that second. She let me drop my bomb in flair and said, "When and where?"

We end up deciding she'll pick up tacos from a food truck nearby and meet at a park a few blocks from her apartment. She's wearing a hoodie, beanie, and jeans, because while sixty-five degrees is practically summer weather to my Wyoming-boy heart, Presley is a California girl. After the last couple days I've had, I want to sit out and enjoy the sun, and she said she was happy to indulge me.

She waves when she meets my eye and hurries toward the picnic table I'm sitting at. I rise to greet her. She sets the food bags on the table and then wraps her arms around my middle, just like she did a couple days ago.

Something about this woman's hugs calm me to the core. I've been buzzing with energy since the game on Thursday, but both times she's hugged me have quieted that buzz to a whisper in my brain.

"You have a meeting?" she asks when she pulls back, but she keeps her hands at my waist, clutching the sides of my long-sleeved shirt like she'll force me to answer now that she's got me in her sights.

I smile and sigh at the same time. The last couple days have been hard, even the moments my agent assured me plenty of teams would want me. There was still an insecurity in all of it that wouldn't let me settle. The niggling thought in my brain that I might be good, great even, at what I do, but my speaking out to the media at the worst possible times outweighs it all. That I was too much of a liability.

"The Rays made an offer," I tell her.

She lets out a tiny squeal that she cuts off, and bounces on her toes. "And?"

I nod at her, and she jumps back into my arms, making me laugh.

"My dad said everyone was going to want you. He said the Rays would make an offer, and I knew you would be so great here." Her words come a mile a minute, and I laugh again. It doesn't stop her. "Brock, you're going to be part of a line that appreciates how good you are."

"I hope so," I say. Truth is I love what she's doing right now. It's pure and sweet, no playing to my ego or anything. That buzzing has turned into a happy energy, and the whispers that I'm on thin ice no matter where I go dissipate in my head.

She gives a light swat to my chest. "No, seriously, Brock. I saw a tweet from *Jett McCombs*. He said he was crossing his fingers the Pumas picked you up because you see everything. Jett. McCombs."

If Jett could hear her now, his head would grow three sizes. Her tone has all the awe that a three-time champion deserves, but it's still funny since we came onto the Pumas together as rookies.

I chuckle. "Jett and I both knew it was a long shot. The Pumas let me go four years ago. It would be strange for them to pick me up again." I shrug like it doesn't mean anything. "Would've been cool to play for them with Jett qb-ing."

She draws in a breath. "Of course you're buddies with him." She slides into a seat at the picnic table. "Well, I'm glad it's the Rays. I'm gonna get you a hoodie right away. And maybe now we can finally beat the Pumas in a playoff game."

I grin at the way her smile turns competitive and sit down across from her. She nudges a bag of tacos toward me and then opens the one in front of her.

"Obviously we're going to beat them." I open my bag and take out a couple of tacos. There are also containers of fresh salsas and veggies. The homemade corn tortillas are stuffed with meat, and it reminds me that Presley gets football life one hundred percent. Even for a lunch out, she's taking the time to get me extra protein and clean foods. I make a note of the name on the bag and commit it to memory to order from again.

"When is your physical?" she asks.

I'll have to be cleared by the Rays' training staff before I can start practice. "Tomorrow morning. They want me ready ASAP."

Her smile widens into her cheeks. "Of course they do." She reaches over the table and grabs my hand, clutching it in hers. "I am so happy you're coming to the Rays, but more than anything, Brock, I'm happy that you're happy." She pulls her hand back to take a bite of her taco. It looks like there are only two in her bag.

Her words burrow into me, and warmth spreads through my chest. I *am* happy. The last couple days were stressful and hard, and some of that energy is still bouncing around inside of me. But most of it has been converted to excitement. The way Lincoln talks about his team, the brotherhood they have, the way they all work together—I've been jealous of that for a while. The Rays have a few all-stars, like Anthony Hurley and Lincoln. Mark Travis, even though he's getting up there in football years. But for the most part, they're a group of good players specifically selected for how they would fit on the team. Look at Eli Dash. He came to them after his worst season with the Arizona Cobras, but now he's playing tight games with the Pumas, the best team in the league.

Lincoln might have put in a good word about me with the coaches, maybe even urged them to take a close look, but in the end, it came down to how I would fit with the specific team they've built. That does something for the hurt feelings I've been carrying most of my life—working my tail off to get a school like USC to notice me, going undrafted and having to try out for a pro team, getting traded by the Pumas for someone "better." It's been adding up, but I need to turn my personal narrative around.

"Thanks, Pres."

She beams at me, lips closed over a mouth full of food, and I dig into my tacos with more gusto than before. They're amazing. Denver has some great taco places, but something about being farther south makes these ones taste that much better.

When we're done eating, we toss our garbage, and I walk Presley back to her apartment. I get a text from Mom while we're walking, and Presley waves at me to answer it.

"She's probably worried about you."

"My mom doesn't worry. She's tough. Had to be."

Presley scoffs. "Sure, she probably told you all the time that she wasn't worried about stuff, but she's a mom. She worries, whether you see it or not. She's probably just better at hiding it than my mom was. Answer her text."

Mom: Look what Kurtis got us! 😄

It's accompanied by a picture of her and Kurtis in yellow Rays sweatshirts. Mom is facing the camera so you can see the Rays logo, and Kurtis is turned around to show "Hunter" across the back.

I tilt the phone and show Presley.

"Oh, I love it!"

"You would." I arch an eyebrow at her.

"Have they been together long?" she asks.

"About a year. He does stuff like this for her all the time." I look at the picture again. I love seeing Mom happy the way she is with him. She's had a fair number of boyfriends over the years. She was careful, especially when I was young, about when to involve them in my life. But as a teen, I always knew when she was dating someone. Flowers and other gifts would show up, or she'd take advantage of football camp to "go see friends." Once I was an adult, she never forced relationships between me and her boyfriends, but she talked more freely about them.

"She looks happy."

"He looks smitten," I agree.

"Absolutely." Presley leans closer to me to look at the picture again, giving it star-eyes.

We arrive at her apartment, and she unlocks the door.

"Are you going to tell me what you were so excited to show me this morning?" I ask.

"Absolutely!" She claps her hands and then gestures for me to follow her inside. "I can't believe I forgot all about it after you said you were in town." I catch a flash of pink to her cheeks before she turns around and disappears into her bedroom.

She comes back a few moments later holding a paper bag. "Prepare yourself," she says with so much faux seriousness I have to swallow back laughter. Hanging out more with Presley is going to be a major plus of playing for the Rays. She's a light in my life that balances my intensity.

She slides a book out of the paper bag, and I recognize it immediately. It's a rare-ish collector's edition of book fifteen, but I'm not sure why she's so excited. She knows I have this same set.

Then she flips open the front page and shows me the signature. My mouth drops open, and I know I've given her the exact reaction she wanted because she bounces again, like she did when she found out the Rays signed me.

"Signed?" I say when she holds out the book for me to inspect. I read the inscription and then look back up at her. "Your aunt met him?"

She throws up her hands. "I guess?" she cries. "She never said *anything*, Brock. I'm thoroughly perplexed about how she would get this and never say anything about it and then just leave it to me when she's dead."

I hand the book back to Presley, and she slips it into the paper bag, setting it on a side table next to her couch. "I feel like I would have liked your aunt a lot."

"Yeah. You would have. It's exasperating that she did this, and I have no answers, but I'm pretty sure she's up there laughing hysterically at me trying to figure this out." Her expression tenses for a moment as she stares at the bag.

I crouch to peer at her. "Pres, it's okay to be mad at her for not telling you."

She shakes her head. "Oh. It's not that. I mean, I'm annoyed, yeah. Because it was probably a great story. Maybe it's in one of the letters she left me, and I have to wait to find out." She sighs. "It's fine."

I pull her into a hug. If there's one thing I've learned from my mom, it's that "fine" doesn't always mean "fine," and there's an edginess to her words that says she feels more than she's letting on. Presley melts into me, putting her face against my chest and wrapping her arms around me. She sighs, and I almost expect her to start crying. She's not afraid to do that with me, something that makes me want to puff out my chest in pride that she trusts me that much. Another lesson my mom drilled into me: tears are normal and nothing to freak out about.

Unless it's because someone hurt her. The same would go for Presley. She's the closest friend I've had in a long time, besides Lincoln, I guess. And even with him, his life has been so busy since he met Layla and then basically became an instant dad.

"It really is okay, Brock. I promise," she says into my chest, but she doesn't make any effort to move.

"If you're sure?" I lean back to look at her. Her cheeks are red, maybe with embarrassment even though she knows crying in front of me is fine.

She steps back and smooths her hair. "Really. Do you want to hang out, or do you need to go?"

"Hang out," I say. Going back to my hotel room would mean thinking too much about everything that's happened this week, even if it ended well. "Should we finish the Christmas movie I slept through?" I suggest, plopping down on her couch.

"Or we could … decorate Christmas cookies?" she says.

I sit up. "I'm in."

She tilts her head toward the kitchen. "I already have every-thing. I made the cookies after work, and I was going to go over to my mom's to decorate until you said you were in town."

I stand and follow her as she moves toward the island that separates her kitchen area from the living room. "I feel bad for taking this opportunity from your mom."

"Don't. I'll go over to her house and decorate again with her sometime. She's big about Christmas too. Where do you think I got it?" She turns away from me, opening her fridge and depositing containers of frosting on the counter. I see the sugar cookies sitting on a cooling rack next to the stove. They're the perfect shade of cream and golden brown on the bottom.

"Those look good," I say, pointing to the cookies as she gathers decorating materials. It's a lot, which shouldn't be surprising since she's told me how much she loves Christmas, and I can tell this is a tradition. She has a kit with frosting bags and tips for different shapes. I take a seat at the island on one of the stools, shifting around until I'm as comfortable as I'm going to get.

"Sorry," Presley says as she watches me. "I don't get many six-seven guys in here."

"I'm used to other people's furniture not being exactly the right size for me. It's like being Goldilocks but the opposite," I joke to make sure she doesn't worry about it.

She brings a tray of cookies over and then takes a seat next to me. She starts chatting about the Rays as she begins spreading a layer of white frosting over a cookie, and I relax into the comfort of our friendship and the lightness to this moment. She turns on some Christmas music to play softly, and I feel settled and comfortable for the first time since Monday night.

I went to my mom's house that night. Packed a bag and left Denver. She was there for me like she has been my whole life, but I couldn't shake the failure that surrounded me in that moment. Mom, Tim, Lincoln, Jett, Presley, everyone assured me from the moment Denver let me go that it was Denver's mistake. Some commentators said it too. Jett texted me as soon as he found out, saying the Devils are trying to right a sinking ship by tossing overboard the only people who care about saving it. I'm grateful for my friends and family and the ways they support me.

So I'm not sure what it is about sitting next to Presley, quietly talking about a dozen different things these last few minutes, that makes the last remnants of that storm inside me die down completely. There's something different about her friendship. I know Jett and Lincoln through football, and to a certain extent that's why Tim is in my life too. So maybe that's it. Maybe it's that she's in a sphere outside of football, and she's not my mom.

Whatever it is, I'm grateful for it and glad I'm going to have it all the time once I move to LA.

CHAPTER 12
PRESLEY

I don't know how I'm able to make coherent conversation. Ever since Brock hugged me when he thought I was upset over Aunt Shannon not telling me about how she got the signature, Mom's words about how we can't stay friends forever are running through my head on repeat.

Friendships like this don't last forever.

One of you is going to meet someone.

I don't know what the single scene is like in Denver, but Brock is a pro-football player. He probably had a ton of opportunities to date beautiful, smart women. Maybe even someone he could introduce TOK to and they might love it.

I can't help thinking those opportunities will double now that he's in LA.

That makes this feel like now or never.

Besides with him moving to LA, shifting this relationship to something more makes sense. The timing is right.

And the fact that Mariah Carey's "All I Want For Christmas Is You" starts playing is like a sign.

Brock is bent over his latest cookie, carefully drawing a red and green football on it. The decorating tools are dwarfed by his large hands, and it's a funny picture. I grab my phone to snap one, and he turns to smile at me, so I take another one before moving to put my phone away.

"Wait a second," he says, reaching for it. "Selfie of us together."

I hand it over, and he uses his extra-long arms to hold out the phone. I lean into him, and since he can hold the phone out so far, he captures both of us, plus the cookies in front of us in the frame. I stare at the picture when I take my phone back from him, warmth filling me.

Maybe this picture will tell a story. *This is the night I told Brock how I felt about him. The rest is history.*

But how exactly do I bring this up? Straightforward seems like the best bet. Spit it out. We've always been honest with each other, so no reason to treat this differently. "Brock," I say tentatively, putting my phone next to me on the counter in case we want some cute photos for after. "I like you."

He turns to me and grins, making my heart flip over. This is a good sign. "Pres," he says. "I like you too."

I'm about to lean forward and seal this surprisingly easy moment with a kiss, but then I stop. That was ... too playful. He's gone right back to his decorating, and with a sinking feeling, I realize he thinks I mean that in a friendly way. Inwardly, I groan.

I put a hand on his arm to pull his attention back to me. "No. I mean ..." I swallow. I don't know how to say this. It's going to come out like we're in middle school. Maybe I should frost a cookie with a heart on it and drag him under the mistletoe.

Mistletoe.

If I kiss him, he'll for sure get the point.

So I stand up. I have to if I'm going to reach his lips, and also that's the easiest way to get closer to him. "Brock?" I say to get his attention. He looks up, and I lean in and press my lips to his, just like that.

His lips are soft and, for a moment, they melt into mine. I grip the sleeve of his shirt. I lean in closer and then—

He pulls back, making me stumble into him. He puts both hands on my arms to straighten me, but also hold me at arm's length.

"Presley," he says. His lips are in a firm line, and when I realize that I'm staring at them, I snap my gaze up to his face. His eyes are wide, and he scoots me another inch away from him.

That's not a good sign.

"I didn't know…" He takes a deep breath. "I mean, when I said I liked you, I thought …"

My cheeks burn. I break out of his grip and take a few steps back, avoiding his gaze as I start moving the cookies I've decorated into a box to take them to work tomorrow. I shouldn't be tempting the players with treats this full of sugar, but hey, it's Christmas. Basically.

"No. I know you didn't mean … that's why … but …" Oh my gosh, there is no good way to have this conversation.

I've ruined everything, just like I thought. And weeks sooner than I needed to, I bet.

I'm going to kill my mom.

"You know what?" I suddenly say, forcing a smile. "It *would* be crazy for something to happen between us." I fumble for a reason besides the fact that he doesn't feel the same way. "Because I'm a trainer on the Rays!" I say it with too much gusto, and Brock's eyebrows jump up. "It would be like …" I search for the word. "Frowned upon." Probably. I don't know that for sure, but it sounds good now.

"Yeah …" He stands and scratches the back of his neck. "So, I'll see you at the facility in the morning?" His tone is awkward and unsure, and I'm so angry at what I've done I could cry.

My throat is actually starting to get thick, and my chest is tight. But even though I've already cried in front of Brock a bunch of times—usually over my aunt, but there was that one time that we were talking about Kael's brother's death—I can't cry in front of him over this. Definitely not.

"Yeah!" I try to sound bright and cheery. "I'm so excited. I can't wait."

Brock steps away from the counter, heading toward the door. "See you later," he says when he puts his hand on the door.

"See you!" I keep my smile firmly in place, waving at him enthusiastically as he slips out. Then I use that same hand to slap myself in the face. I'm so stupid. I didn't even get a chance to tell him about the ring I found and what he thinks I should do. He was the only one I could tell and now …?

I run directly to my room, throw myself on my bed, and let my tears free.

CHAPTER 13

BROCK

It's been almost a full day since I spoke to Presley in any form, and I hate it. We haven't gone this long without talking to each other in some way since the first couple weeks after we met. We saw each other when I came into the facility for my physical this morning, but our only contact was her fake happy wave, the same one she gave me when I left her apartment last night, and by the time I got done with the team doctor, she wasn't in the training room anymore.

Her cookies were.

Well, our cookies. I saw the box sitting on one of the tables in the training room with a note in her handwriting for everyone to help themselves. When I looked inside, I noticed she'd packed up the ones I'd decorated as well. I didn't eat one last night since I left early, so I took advantage. And I felt guilty with every bite.

I lectured Lincoln about not saying anything that would make her think our friendship was more than it was, and yet somehow I ended up doing exactly that. How stupid of me to tell her I liked her too. It seemed like such an innocent thing for her to say, to express her contentment with our friendship, that my answer came automatically. I was feeling the same thing, I thought. Gratitude for those moments together and how easy it was to be together.

Then she kissed me.

I was so surprised, I kissed her back. It came automatically, like Presley and I kissed all the time. I can't explain why my lips did that before I pulled away. It kind of just happened.

Maybe she kissed me on accident, and we can put this behind us?

I groan to myself as I make my way to my rental car in the facility parking lot. I totally blew up my friendship with Presley by unknowingly leading her on. There's no fixing this.

On the bright side, the doctor said I was in great shape and he'd have me cleared for practice tomorrow. I'm eager to start working with the team, seeing where I fit.

Should I text Presley and tell her the good news? Act normal, like we didn't kiss last night and she didn't confess that she likes me romantically?

But acting normal and allowing our friendship to grow like it did is what got me in this mess in the first place. I think of our hugs and how I found comfort in them. It's not Presley's fault she read into them. It didn't even cross my mind at the time that they might feel like more to her.

I spend the afternoon arranging to have my stuff moved to LA. For now I'll put it in a storage unit until I find a permanent place to stay. The nice thing about having money is that moving isn't a pain. It makes the process of changing teams easier, which is something I need. When that's all done, I head down to the gym at the hotel and hop on a treadmill. I need to run off some energy and distract myself from thinking about how I was going to ask Presley if she wanted to help me house hunt.

Maybe I could text her to ask if she knows a good real estate agent. That's pretty much business, and if I keep our texts to that kind of thing and talk about TOK, I can avoid leading her on even more. More than anything, I don't want Presley to think I'm playing games with her.

But asking her about houses could also seem domestic. Intimate.

I growl as I increase the speed on the treadmill. Can I really not figure out a way to fix this?

As I finish up my five-mile run, Lincoln texts, telling me to come over for dinner. I'm grateful for the invitation. My evening was stretching out wide in front of me with nothing to do except study the new playbook. And considering I screwed up my relationship with Presley, Lincoln is my only friend in LA. Lincoln's neighborhood has exploded with Christmas decorations since I was here last. Most of the houses have classy, understated decorations with simple lights and wreaths, but I pass one with a lawn crowded with a blow up Santa, reindeer, snowmen, and even a nativity.

Margot is already down for bed by the time I get to Lincoln's, which is disappointing. The steak and roasted vegetables meal is plated and sitting on the dining room table for us, probably left by the chef that comes in to cook for them. Both Layla and Lincoln have specific diets, so it's a lot easier for them if someone else plans it out and executes it. When I was in Denver, there was a woman I hired regularly during the season. I put that on my mental list to get arranged for here in LA.

Is that something innocent I can text Presley about to clear the air? The tacos she chose yesterday were delicious, even if what happened after the meal was disastrous. She's clearly familiar with my dietary needs and might know someone who is as well.

I can just as easily ask someone on the team, and she knows that.

I put her out of my mind. I came over here as a distraction and to stop replaying those awkward moments in Presley's apartment last night.

"So," Lincoln says once we're all eating. "Something happened with you and Presley." He studies me as he stabs a piece of steak with his fork.

So much for distraction.

"Nothing happened," I say quickly, but my heated cheeks are like a siren that something did happen, just not what Lincoln probably thinks.

"*Something* did." Lincoln waves the bite of steak around. "Every time I said your name today, she got this fake-looking smile on her face, and she changed the subject as quickly as possible. The cookies were great, by the way."

I rub my hand across my face. "I didn't make them. Just helped decorate."

"Explain," Lincoln says, his voice the slightest bit stern, like he doesn't mean for it to come out that way but he can't help it. It's probably protectiveness. Presley's a part of their Tuesday gossip session and quilting bee or whatever because they're all in the facility at the same time that day.

"Presley told me … she has feelings for me. And…" I trail off because she never said that, only that she liked me, which is what she meant. It was the kiss that explained. "She, uh, kissed me. And then I had to tell her … I don't feel the same." It's as difficult to explain now as it was last night when Presley and I fumbled around for words.

Lincoln's eyes widen, and he shares a look with Layla. Some unspoken conversation happens before they both turn back to me. "And … that kiss was really just … nothing?" Lincoln asks.

Of course it wasn't nothing. It was a big, fat bomb to our friendship. It blew everything up because Presley thought I wanted to kiss her.

"We're just friends—I mean, I *thought* we were just friends. I clearly did something to make Presley believe it was more, and now our friendship is probably ruined."

Layla squints at me, her fork hovering over the pile of perfectly seasoned roasted vegetables on her plate. "So you didn't feel anything? No spark?" She sounds confused, like I told her Margot was an ugly baby. That's preposterous, and we all know it.

"No?" I look back and forth between Lincoln and Layla. The kiss happened so fast there wasn't anything to feel except surprise.

Lincoln smirks. "That sounds like a question."

"Don't you think I'd know if I felt that way about Presley? Wouldn't the sparks be obvious?" I'd want to spoil her the way Kurtis is always showering my mom with his time, attention, and gifts, like flowers and trips. I wouldn't be able to keep my eyes and hands off her, like Tim and Meg.

Layla shrugs. "I guess the sparks were obvious for me once I started paying attention, but I was so intent on *not* feeling anything that I kind of ignored what I thought was just friendship."

Lincoln laughs before giving his wife that adoring look that makes me happy for him—and jealous at the same time. "I was in love with her the first time I saw her."

She snorts. "That's ridiculous. You didn't even know me."

He plants a light kiss on her lips. "Didn't need to."

"Ahh, so it was all superficial," she teases.

"The first time I saw you, you were holding Margot," he says like that's all the explanation he needs to give. It works though, because Layla's eyes go soft, and she gazes at him with the same love he stares at her with.

Yeah, I would definitely know if I felt *this* way about Presley. Even *I* can feel the chemistry between Lincoln and Layla right now, so surely I'd know if it was happening to me.

But the truth is … I don't remember what I felt when she kissed me. Like I said, everything happened so quickly. Her mouth was on mine, and it was soft and nice—

Okay, that explains it. You don't think a kiss is just nice if you felt a spark, right? It should feel like fire, and I didn't feel fire.

"Brock?" Lincoln's voice pulls me from my thoughts. He and Layla stare at me expectantly.

"Uh, yeah?"

He raises an eyebrow, like *explain that*, but I shake my head. It's not what he thinks.

"What?" I ask.

"It's just … like with Natasha—"

"We've already talked about this. It was different."

"And you're not distracted now?" he argues. "You have a lot on your plate, and you have for weeks. Maybe you did start out as friends, but all the stuff with the Devils is overshadowing what's there."

I sigh, thinking of all the ways I've seen my friends and family show their love. Even Jett, when everything in him told him to stay away from Ava, he couldn't ignore his obvious feelings for her. "Why am I not finding excuses to see her all the time, the way you went to Layla's food truck?" Lincoln has the decency to turn red when I remind him of how he bought desserts he could never eat while he was trying to get up the nerve to ask her out. "If I was in love with her, I'd want to kiss her the moment she walks into a room, wouldn't I?"

"Everyone loves differently, Brock," Layla says. "That's why there are books and books and books about the psychology of it."

"I'd know," I insist.

"So that's it?" Lincoln asks. "Your great friendship with Presley is just over?"

Something heavy drops into my stomach. I've been dreading facing this thought since last night. I hate the idea of not having her in my life.

"No," I reply automatically. "We can still be friends."

Layla and Lincoln share another one of those couple looks. "For now," Lincoln says slowly. "You can't be book besties when she's married to someone else."

I open my mouth to retort that it's about books so why not but can't say it.

Layla snaps her fingers a couple times. "What's his name?

From the wedding. I think you said he plays for the Cobras now?"

"Brendan Tanner," Lincoln says. I tense. He was a receiver, like Lincoln, who played at USC with us. I don't talk much to him now, so I can't explain why I don't like where I think Layla's going with this.

"We should set her up with him. She could probably convince him to read those books." She whips her head toward me. "What's the name of them?"

I blink at her and stare for several seconds. "I know what you guys are doing."

Layla's eyes are the picture of innocence. She *is* an actress, and a very good one. "What?"

"Trying to make me jealous. Also TOK is not something you convince people to like." I should've stopped talking before I said that. It does sound jealous. Even I hear it. Like no one could possibly share the bond Presley and I have over those books because we've both loved them since childhood.

The thing is no one likes TOK, and it's not going to suddenly become popular after twenty years.

"Listen." My tone is defensive, and Lincoln bites his lips together, probably to keep from laughing at me. "Okay, you and Eli and his sister all ended up with people you were friends with first, but it doesn't mean that every time a man and a woman are friends that romance is around the corner."

Amusement is written all over Lincoln's face. He holds up his hands in surrender. "So you and Presley are going to go back to being friends—for now." It's like he can't help but add that. "As soon as you get past the awkward. Sounds great."

I sigh and go back to eating. He doesn't get it. Fine. He's not matchmaking, so I'll be grateful for that and figure out how to fix my friendship with Presley.

It's *fine*.

CHAPTER 14

PRESLEY

I've picked up my phone at least a dozen times since I got home from work to text Brock. It's so natural to check in with him on all the little things that happen with my day, but after last night, everything I send is going to sound flirty or like I'm trying to convince him to like me back.

So now I have a private window open on my web browser, searching every article about the Christmas ring in hopes of distracting myself from the dumpster fire I've made of my friendship with Brock.

I miss him.

I miss him so much, and it's only been a day of no contact.

This might be why I have a sad love song playing on repeat on my phone, and every time it gets to the chorus about never getting to talk to their ex again, I sing it at the top of my lungs with what I feel like is some serious emotion and believable heartbreak.

It's even clearer to me now how hard I fell for him, how much our friendship meant to me, and how heartbreaking it is that he doesn't want more. For a few seconds, our kiss was electric. I could have melted into him. I drift into a daydream where instead of him yanking away from me so quickly like he did, he pulls me *to* him, wrapping his arms around my back. I shiver at the thought and then scowl.

No, Presley. No. That's not going to happen.

But do I *truly* regret the kiss?

Mostly, yes. Okay, probably fifty-fifty.

"Back to the task at hand, girl." I focus my concentration on the news articles I've found about the Christmas ring. How in the world did Aunt Shannon end up with the ring in her possession? I've tried image searching to see if there were replicas out there and maybe this is one of them, but everything I can find is about the stolen ring. Even searching for Westcott Christmas ring replica doesn't lead to anything but some Facebook posts about Mrs. Westcott's attempts to find the ring among her neighbors. That was funny.

Can the NSA spy on my private internet searches? Probably. And this doesn't look good for me if they do. They'd start asking questions like why do I have it? And why am I so interested in having a duplicate? And why haven't I turned it in if I'm innocent?

I need advice about what to do, but I don't know who to call. Mom will make me turn it in but having Aunt Shannon's name dragged through the mud will break her heart. It's best if she doesn't know. Brock is the only other person I trust enough. I have friends from high school and college, but they're not that kind of friends. Mom and Aunt Shannon were my best friends once I moved back to LA after college and, truth be told, I didn't try very hard to find friends my age. I was always with Mom and Aunt Shannon. I go out with my friends from time to time, but none of those relationships are the kind where you confess you're pretty sure you're in possession of stolen property.

I've listed out everything I can remember from the Westcott's Christmas party, but there's not much since Aunt Shannon died unexpectedly a couple days later. Things that happened just before her death are either in crystal clear focus or completely blurred from my mind.

Sifting through the pictures Mom, Aunt Shannon, and I posted on social media that night has helped me piece things together. The bottom line is that I don't remember a time period long enough where Aunt Shannon could have ditched me, Mom, Dad, and Thomas to go steal the ring from the safe at the Westcott's house. Their long staircase would've made it next to impossible. Aunt Shannon could still walk on her own, but navigating stairs? It would have taken her forever to do by herself.

So … someone else had to have taken it, and then Aunt Shannon somehow got it. Could Thomas have been in on it? He was making jokes about it …

No, there's no way. He's like family. He's an FBI agent and a straight arrow. He would never.

My hand falls to my phone again, itching to call Brock.

I pull my hand back. What would he even say? He doesn't have any special expertise that's suddenly going to help in this situation. I just want to talk to him.

I bury my face in my hands and let out a growl of frustration. Then I take a deep breath and go back to my computer. I open Facebook to check out Aunt Shannon's friends. I'll know most of them, so the ones I don't, maybe I can look up. If I'm lucky, one of them will be the obvious thief. They must have stashed the ring at Aunt Shannon's house, coincidentally in the box she was leaving for me. The boxes were stored in her bedroom closet. It would have looked like any random storage box.

That makes sense.

I click on my notifications out of habit. I'm not on Facebook a lot, but it's where the main fan group for TOK is. I'm derailed from my purpose by wondering if Brock is in the fan group. I've never seen him comment or post anything. He could have joined under a pseudonym if he didn't want people to troll him. He has an official Facebook fan page that I assume is run by someone else since none of the posts sound like Brock at all.

Yes, I've checked.

I can't help it. I click on the TOK page and then on the

members of the group. There are around a hundred people in the fan group, so it's easy to scroll through and find Brock's name. He's on Facebook as Brock Bennett Hunter with his middle name (his mom's maiden name, he told me once). Unless you're a big football fan, you wouldn't put it together. His face is more recognizable than his name, thanks to the memes. His picture is the most hilarious thing. It must be from high school. I can see Brock in the shape of his face, but he doesn't have a beard, and his hair is longer, slicked back like he's some kind of villain. I snort. I follow Brock on Instagram—that's where we connect on social media from time to time—and he definitely isn't posting pictures like this. I'm *so* tempted to screenshot it and send it to him. Two days ago, I wouldn't have even thought twice. Now it'll look like I'm stalking him.

I click on his name, and sure enough it shows me that he hasn't interacted with any of the posts on the page. He's a lurker, and I love it because that fits.

I click back into the main discussion page even though I'm pretty sure I'm caught up on TOK news. I was on last week, and the last post was two weeks old.

A post from the admin has taken its spot though. It's been shared from the official TOK page on Facebook, and the admin's only comment is a line of exclamation points.

FOR GOOD REASON.

The headline of the post teases something about the sixteenth book. I click frantically on the original post so I can read more than the first couple lines.

Shadow Quill Publishing announces the release of Veil of the Queen, *the sixteenth and final book in the Obsidian Kingdom series. It will be released on December 1ˢᵗ.*

What?! It's happening. There's going to be a book. This is official, from the *official* page, which only ever publishes true TOK news, never any of the theories or speculation. The article goes on to talk about a special release event at a bookstore in New York City, and the first twenty-five people in line to buy the book will be able to attend a small gathering with Gideon Thornridge.

I click on the link and purchase two tickets for the event without even thinking about it. Brock and I will still have to get there early to make sure we're one of the first twenty-five—that shouldn't be too hard with so few die-hard fans anyway.

I check the calendar next, squealing with delight to see that the event is on a Tuesday, Brock's day off. It will be a brutal day for us, and he'll pay for it in practice the next day since we'll be in late, but worth it. I'll have to rearrange a few things because I typically work with the guys on their days off—

I've made most of the plans in my head before I remember Brock and I are … I don't even know what we are right now. In a really awkward place?

But this is TOK! This is exactly why we have to stay friends, and I need to fix this right now. I don't hesitate this time to snatch up my phone to text him.

Presley: BROCK.
Presley: Grandma is all out today. YOU HAVE TO SEE THIS.

I add a link to the announcement on Facebook so he knows right away what I'm talking about and doesn't think this is some desperate attempt on my part to get him to like me romantically. It is a desperate attempt to get him to stay my friend, but clearly our friendship is meant to be even if something more never works out. This announcement the day after our big, awkward moment? The book release falling on his day off so we can attend? It's fate making sure we stay together.

Well, not *together* together. Just friends together.

I stare at the screen and wait for his response, and pretty soon the bubbles pop up and bounce. Then they disappear. Then they bounce again. Then they disappear.

How is this a hard thing to respond to? Even with the

awkwardness. I decide to nip all of it in the bud so we can enjoy this moment.

Presley: Listen, I'm sorry about last night. I was crazy and I don't want our friendship to crash and burn over this. Can we forget it happened?

The bubbles bounce some more, and I growl again. I shake my phone like I want to be shaking Brock by the shoulders. It wouldn't be very effective at shaking sense into him since I would barely move him, and I'd look ridiculous with how far up I'd have to reach, but the intent would be clear.

Finally, a text pops up.

Brock: The last thing I want to do is hurt you. I don't want to risk leading you on when I know how you feel.

I have to convince him it's going to be fine. My feelings don't matter. I'm sure I can move on and make them go away anyway. I send him a GIF of someone looking innocent.

Presley: Not sure what you're talking about? How I feel? Like the fact that I think you're insane to believe that Thornridge is going to unveil Lyra as the Obsidian Queen? 🫤

Brock: 😅 Presley…

Presley: Let's not make this a thing. I was drunk on eggnog and said some silly things. It's behind us both. Please please please forget it and go to New York with me so we can wait in line and SEE GIDEON THORNRIDGE.

Brock: 😄 We weren't drinking eggnog.

Presley: That's not how I remember it. Truth be told, the whole night is a blur. Really fuzzy.

Brock: 🙍

Presley: I already bought the tickets. Are you going to waste

yours on my dad, who only *pretends* to like TOK, because you had some weird eggnog-induced dream?
Brock: Are you gaslighting me?
Presley: Is it working?
…

…

Brock: Court's aunt has connections. Eli can get us a private jet. I'll take care of it.

I cry out in triumph and jump up on my bed. "Yes!" I pump my fist in the air. I have Brock back, and it's not everything I want but it's enough if I get to keep him for now.

I notice the private tab for the ring search I was doing earlier and scowl at the screen. Then I shut my laptop. This can definitely wait another day.

CHAPTER 15
BROCK

Trying to be just friends with Presley is a bad idea. I'll have to watch everything I say and do and make sure I don't give her the wrong idea. I can't lead her on again and hurt her. It's selfish to try this, but I can't say no to her. And there's TOK to think about. The new book is coming out, dropping lightning fast in a way that's generated some buzz about it among more than just the TOK community. Book influencers on social media are talking about the surprise announcement for the "little known classic," and the TOK fan pages have been flooded with reviews for the first book that new readers are posting as they start the series. And they like it. They're calling it "cool in a quirky way," which tells me they don't get it. In any case, the book release event has sold out, and Presley and I will need to get to the bookstore earlier than we thought if we're going to score tickets to the gathering with the author.

Meanwhile, today is my first game with the Rays. I don't expect a lot of playing time. I've only had a few practices with the team this week, but I'm nervous anyway. I have to prove I'm worth the drama.

In my first meeting with the coach, I promised him I wouldn't let my emotions rule my mouth. He'd chuckled, put a hand on my shoulder, and said, "I'm hoping you don't have any drama to spill here, Hunter. And if you do, I hope you'll spill it to me first."

He reminds me of Tim—a coach who wants to get to know me, who isn't letting memes rule his opinion of me, and who will make sure I get a fair shot.

Maybe that's why I feel double pressure to prove myself to him. Especially when he puts me in the first offensive play of the game.

Lincoln grins at me and gives me a hard pat on the shoulder as we huddle up for the play. My nerves settle back a notch, knowing I've got him watching my back. It's more than I had at the Devils.

I set up on the line, my heart pumping. The crowd is a low hum, and I push the noise to the background. I scan the linebackers opposite me on the defense for the Cobras. My brain stops on number sixty-five, the defensive end lined up opposite me. There's something off about where he is. I catalogue it and ready myself for the count.

Jett McCombs has praised me for being able to see the little details, and that's because during plays, time seems to slow for me. It's like I'm a little bit of The Flash, everyone around me moving slower while my brain works faster. They're blitzing on the first play, probably trying to put Eli on edge. I move quickly to block the end coming in, knocking into him hard and shouting to point out the linebacker rushing in. Mark Travis, the Rays tight end, shifts quickly into place to block him. In my peripheral, I see Eli toss the ball toward Baker, the wide receiver on his right who's uncovered because the Cobras sent most of their guys to the left. Baker gets an easy first down before the defenders chase him out of bounds.

"Nice spot!" Travis yells at me as we jog back to the huddle. He pounds my helmet—not a great feeling but I grin anyway.

Lincoln shoves at my side. "Thought they were going to sneak through Hunter's side? They haven't watched their film."

He laughs, and the whole team nods in agreement. The Cobras thought they could take advantage of my first time on the field as a Ray. I grin at the praise, my nerves settling even more. On the sideline, the coach is clapping his hands, and he points at me. I read, "Nice one," off his lips before I turn back to my team.

We start marching up the field, and a few plays later, I notice the linebackers are off again, this time on the right side.

As soon as Eli finishes his count and the ball is snapped, I shout down the line, "They're coming, they're coming!" I hold my position, yelling at the offensive line as the blitz comes in. Lincoln manages to get a couple yards. It's not much, but it's enough for a first down.

We end up kicking a field goal, but it's a good first drive to the game. Excitement pulses through me. It's the best drive I've been a part of in a long time. I find Lincoln on the sidelines once the defense has taken the field.

"Johnson is lining up a hair over his gap when they're blitzing," I tell him.

Lincoln shakes his head in awe at me. "You always did notice the little things. Allen is going to get jealous," he says, speaking of the Rays center, Shawn Allen. "Why're you telling me and not him?"

My brows come down. It's obvious. "Because I know you. I trust you."

Lincoln leans toward me. "Here?" He gestures around him at the players on the sidelines. "You can trust everyone." I can't help my skeptical look. Lincoln claps me on the shoulder. "I promise, Hunter. And you said you trusted me." He shoves me toward Allen.

I stride over, my smile growing with each second. This is how football is supposed to be.

CHAPTER 16
PRESLEY

When the game is over, I want to run up to Brock, throw my arms around him, and tell him how proud I am of him. He was so *awesome*. I was working among all the guys during the game, so I heard the way they talked about him, the way the offensive line praised his sharp eyes and laser instincts. I beamed every time I heard it.

But I have to be just-friend Presley, and that means watching my every move.

Still, when he walks up to me, his grin so wide it could power the stadium, I start to open my arms. It's natural. As instinctual as the way Brock has a sixth sense for when someone's moving in on his quarterback. I quickly drop my arms and content myself with throwing all my pride into my smile.

For a half second, Brock leans toward me, and then he straightens, shaking himself a little.

"That was amazing," I say, turning so that I'm walking down the sidelines with him toward the tunnel and the locker room. I've got a couple guys I need to check on, but I want to make sure I spend a minute telling Brock how cool he is. That's what friends do. It doesn't mean anything more.

"Thanks, Pres. It felt amazing."

I almost reach up to squeeze his elbow, then stop myself. This is harder than I thought. "Everyone loves you."

"Probably not everyone."

"I'm pretty sure it was everyone."

He stops arguing. He leans sideways, like he might bump into me, but then shuffles away. "Sorry," he mumbles. "Must be tired."

He does look tired, and he played so hard, obviously trying to prove to the team that they didn't make a mistake picking him up.

Maybe that's why we fall into a weird silence as we continue walking together. Normally, Brock and I would have so much to talk about it would be hard to walk away from him to do my job. I want to tell him about the ring, but this isn't the place. If the other night hadn't happened, and I hadn't screwed things up, we'd probably have some shorthand way to discuss it now and how I've been trying to find people through Aunt Shannon's Facebook who might have set her up.

Ugh. Why is this so hard?

I should have never said anything about my feelings, just suffered in silence, like a good romance-novel heroine. "Well," I say the same time he says, "So …"

I rush on. "I'm sorry. I gotta go do PT stuff. See you Tuesday morning?"

He waves me off with a happy expression I can tell is a little fake. "Bright and early."

I give him what I hope is a teammate-like pat on the pads and then hurry into the tunnel. We'll be spending the entire day together on Tuesday. Will it end up in disaster?

————

TALKING IS EASIER Sunday and Monday nights via text as we make the arrangements for the book signing. The flight is about five hours, and book sales at the little bookstore where it will be releasing start at noon. Brock and I both agreed that an hour early should be plenty to get the tickets to the gathering, but with the time difference, it means our flight is taking off at one a.m.

Brock has made all the travel arrangements, not giving me many details other than he'll pick me up at my apartment, and that our ride from Teterboro Airport to the bookstore in Queens is taken care of. He won't let me chip in any money for it either.

You bought the tickets, he texted when I argued about it. Those were cheap compared to everything he's arranging.

I got a couple hours of sleep but I don't know if that's better considering I'm loopy enough to forget I have to be just-friend Presley now, and I cry, "Oh, I love you," when he hands me a coffee cup. Then I widen my eyes. "I was talking to the coffee," I say quickly.

"Gingerbread latte," he says.

I press my lips together before I again confess my love for him and can't cover it up. "You are awesome." I pat him on the shoulder like I did at the game. His warmth spreads across my hand, shooting straight up my arm and to my heart. I can be his friend. I can. *I can*. This will be my mantra, and I will ignore any such warmth that touching him creates.

"You're welcome." He steps into the apartment and puts his hands in his pockets. He stays just a few steps inside. It's only the third time he's been here, but the other two times he made himself comfortable on the couch pretty much right away.

"You ready?" he asks.

I grab my travel bag from the floor by the couch. I'm bringing the collector's book Aunt Shannon got for me. If we get to meet Gideon Thornridge today, I'm going to try asking him about the book. He's signed so few books, there's a chance he'll remember my aunt. I also have a small blanket tucked inside my bag, since planes are always cold. I'm wearing my stretchy, super comfy wide-leg jeans and my Straight Outta Eldraeth hoodie. (The fan merch you can find in the forum is seriously top notch.) I grab my coat, sit down to pull on my tennis shoes, then pop back up.

"Ready."

"Nice hoodie," Brock says with a smirk. He shifts back his black jacket to reveal a t-shirt that says, "Plot twist: *I'm* the Obsidian Queen."

I snort with laughter. "So perfect."

His smirk widens to a grin. "I know." For a tiny moment everything is the same as it always was between us, and I almost sigh with contentment. I get ahold of myself so I don't ruin this small piece of us and pick up my coffee from the side table to head downstairs.

An SUV idles next to the curb with a driver waiting for us. I look over at Brock, one eyebrow raised at this flex.

"Easier than parking a car," he grunts and opens the door for me.

"Not complaining." I slip in and across the seat, and then realize we have to take such a large vehicle because Brock literally couldn't fold himself into anything smaller. His head is almost brushing the ceiling, and his knees are pulled uncomfortably close to him. And listen, it's by no doing of mine that despite me sitting in the normal place one would behind the driver, my arm is brushing Brock's. He just takes up that much space. He's huge, and I rarely notice it except in moments like this.

"You should've sat in front," I say to him. "More leg room."

"This is fine." He shrugs, and our arms brush again.

Be cool, Presley. The electricity enveloping my whole body from that one brush is not a big deal. I look out the window and sip the delicious latte he brought me.

"Where's your coffee?" I ask when I realize he's not holding a cup.

"I don't drink caffeine." He pulls a water bottle from the backpack at his feet.

"Goodie-goodie."

He bursts into laughter. "This is a fine-tuned machine, Pres," he says, ever-so-seriously.

It is a *very fine* tuned machine. To cover for the way I was checking him out, I reach across him and grab his backpack, pulling it over to rest on my side.

"I have plenty of room for this." I take another sip of my latte and stare ahead.

Brock shifts and then moves his arm across the top of the seat, but he makes sure he's not touching me with any part of his arm. "Sorry," he says, and something passes between us. An admission that he knows how this looks, and he feels bad he's initiating it when he was so worried about leading me on. "It's just a really small car."

That comment is what makes everything okay because the lightness to our conversation is real. "It's not a small car at all, Brock," I say. "It's an Escalade. It's one of the biggest SUVs out there."

"It feels small." He shifts again, trying unsuccessfully to sit further onto his side.

In that moment, we could be riding in a tiny, two-door clown car and it wouldn't be any more suffocating than the way it feels right now. The space in here is packed full of the feelings for him I shouldn't have and the weight of his rejection.

"We could be riding in a Humvee and you'd be cramped." I lean my head against my window. How isn't the presence of us in this car pressing in on Brock the way it is on me? It would be much easier if I could scoot close to him and nestle underneath his arm. Close my eyes and fall asleep against him.

I shake the daydream off and force a smile. This is going to be a long day.

———

Flying private is amazing. Security is a breeze, and the plane is simple, yet gorgeous. The leather of the seats is buttery. There are four single chairs, two on each side of the plane, and they swivel so they can face each other. There's also a love seat and a small bar taking up the back part of the seating section. Brock sits in one of the single chairs, and I sit in the one that's already swiveled to face him. I busy myself with pulling out my blanket and rummaging in my backpack for my headphones as the plane prepares for takeoff, and we're both quiet. I'm hoping it has to do with the early morning hour rather than still being uncomfortable around each other.

Once I'm situated, I stare out the window and try to think of a conversation topic that will put us back on even footing. Obviously anything about TOK. Without any awkwardness, we can speculate all day long about what we think will be in book sixteen. We can argue about how Brock thinks the black ring that grants Lyra her power is *the* Obsidian Ring that makes her identity as the Obsidian Queen obvious.

Listen, I can see how he might get there. But isn't that a little too obvious? Right? Thornridge is a better writer than that.

The ring.

I can ask him what he thinks I should do about the Christmas ring.

That's perfect. I can pick up on the conversation I planned to have with Brock before the Christmas Cookie Debacle.

I turn from the window to look at him. "Brock, what level would you say our friendship is?"

There's panic in his eyes for a moment, but he smooths it out. I hear how that could have sounded, considering what happened last week, but I don't address it.

"How are we measuring?" he asks in an indifferent tone.

"From you'd like my post on Instagram to you'd bury a body with me." Before I tell him everything, it's definitely important to know if he'll support me in slightly criminal activity.

"Who else in your life would actually be as well-equipped as me to carry a body for you?" His lips twitch, and I struggle to keep a straight face.

See. When we can ignore the silly thing I did, our friendship is great. But also, the way he went right to that joke? Heart flutters.

Why, Brock Hunter? Why can't you fall in love with me?

"Good point," I say, instead of indulging the urge to beg him to love me. "So we're saying we're at bury a body level?"

"Absolutely."

I look down at my lap and tap my fingers against my bag. "And you wouldn't be bothered if I admitted to *mild* criminal activity." I look up in time to catch his eyebrows jumping.

His expression stays chill, but the amusement leaves. "I know you well enough to trust that any mild criminal activity you'd participate in is probably justified."

I let out a sigh. "It is. And it's Aunt Shannon's fault."

He leans forward, but a flight attendant interrupts to ask us to buckle our seatbelts so we can take off. Brock sits back again, and we do as we're asked. We wait until the attendant has left before we speak again.

"How did your aunt rope you into criminal activity?"

"She stole a ring. Or she held on to a ring for someone who stole it." The words come in a rush of need to have someone else in on this when I haven't been able to say anything. To have *Brock* in on this, the person I've come to trust as much as I did Aunt Shannon herself. "I don't know because she left it in my box to take care of."

He tilts his head, his expression clearly saying, "Go on."

So I do. I tell him about how the Christmas ring was stolen from the Westcott's party a year ago and how I found it.

"It would have been impossible for her to have stolen it herself," I explain. "It was upstairs in a safe, and even if she knew how to break into a safe, she couldn't have made it up the stairs without help. I don't know how she got it or why she has it or why she left it with me, and I don't know what to do."

"And you want to know why," he says in a low voice.

"I don't want to turn it in and have Aunt Shannon blamed for stealing it when I don't have any answers for how she might have gotten it." I twist the fabric of my bag, wishing Brock has some magic answer for me.

He reaches across the space between us, takes my hand, and squeezes it. "We'll figure it out."

I relax, and I believe him. He doesn't have an answer, but he's there for me. And that's enough, I think, for me. It doesn't have to be more.

The lies I tell myself.

"Brock?" I squeeze his hand back in gratitude. "I'd totally bury a body with you too."

CHAPTER 17
BROCK

As we drive from Teterboro Airport to the bookstore, I stare out the window at the flashes of red and green Christmas lights and decorations along the street, anything but thinking too much about the warmth of Presley's head resting on my shoulder and how it shouldn't be as comfortable as it is. Things have been back and forth with us since I picked her up, moments like this where it's like our friendship never changed and then other times when we're overthinking everything we do. When she told me about her aunt and the ring, it was natural to reach out for her. It wasn't until after, when our conversation slowed—probably sleepiness on my part—that I thought about it more closely and wondered if I had given her mixed signals about my real feelings. She'd definitely be confused if she knew that I liked the way she was leaning into me, almost like she's letting me take care of her. To be fair, Presley did start out with her head leaned back against the head rest when she first fell asleep and slowly her head shifted until it rested against my shoulder.

Our five-hour flight was uneventful, and the private jet Eli arranged for us was nice. But neither of us really slept. Presley claimed the caffeine was keeping her awake. I'm sure thoughts about what to do with the ring kept her up as well. We brainstormed some things, but Presley's mostly thought of everything, and it always circles back to how to get it to the police or the Westcotts without anyone knowing it was ever in Presley's or her aunt's possession. I suggested her mailing it, but she's sure that fingerprints or something will lead them back to her. We're both stumped.

So when that conversation died, Presley took out book fifteen, which she's already halfway done with. I have no idea how she got through the last four books in such a short amount of time. I listened to two on audiobooks at ridiculously fast speeds and still only got through book thirteen before I grabbed a couple hours of sleep last night. The last few in the series are crazy long. I'm eager to see how long book sixteen will be. Thornridge has a lot of plotlines to wrap up, and if Lyra is revealed as the Obsidian Queen, he'll need to do a lot of explaining. The press releases have given away nothing, not the blurb or even the cover. Everything will be a surprise to fans when they show up today, and the internet is freaking out over it. The release even made headlines on some of the bigger news sites the last couple days. It's the most hype TOK has ever gotten, and I'm sure the publicists behind it all planned everything in hopes this would play out exactly like it is.

Presley gives a little sigh, reminding me that her cheek is squished against my arm. I want to snap a picture of how cute she looks with her lips pushed out a little bit, but I'd have to move to get my phone from my pocket and that would wake her up.

She'd be so much more comfortable if I could put my arm around her and pull her against me, but selfish as it is to be Presley's friend, I can't go further and do things like that to toy with her. Taking her hand this morning was too far. I mean these actions innocently, and she'd understand that, but it wouldn't help our situation.

The thing is, despite Presley not being my typical type, she is beautiful. Her thick brown hair is braided over her shoulder, and her long lashes rest against her cheeks. The fact that we're just friends isn't because she's not attractive to me—she is.

It's that I would know, right? There would be *something*.

I stare down at her, paying close attention to everything I feel. I can admit that Lincoln's not wrong that, when seen from the outside, Presley and I make sense romantically. We talk a lot, text, and share the details of our lives. We're comfortable with each other, and our close friendship makes the hand holding and hugs and her sleeping on my shoulder natural. Plus I love spending time with her. I'm grateful to be here with her, and I'm glad she pushed for us to do this together and made it happen. I'm also grateful to have found someone who shares the books that were so important to me growing up along with loving the sport that I love. Plus, she was amazing when everything went down with the Devils. She was understanding and thoughtful, and even though I could tell she was concerned and wanted more information from me, she never pushed.

There's warmth in my chest as I think about how kind she is to me, but it's not that spark of fire I'd expect if I wanted more of a relationship. Not the zing that should be here. Would I like kissing her?

I picture it—as an experiment. Me, pushing that stray hair that's fallen from her braid away from her cheek. Her eyes expectant, like they were the night she told me she liked me, as she tilts her chin up toward me. I would lean in closer, touch my lips to hers while she smiles with anticipation—

The Escalade stops at the curb in front of the bookstore, The Sorcery Shop, ending the imaginary moment abruptly. I straighten when I realize I've leaned toward Presley. See, that proves it. No butterflies or anything.

Not that I actually pictured kissing her, but I got close. I would have felt something.

The bookstore is tiny, and according to the internet, the owner is one of the biggest TOK fans out there. She started most of the Reddit threads, and she's a regular contributor to the Facebook fan page and the website forum. The door is on the right side of the shop, and a big window is on the left. There's a sign announcing the release of *Veil of the Queen* and the exclusive sale here at this store until Christmas. There are window drawings of Christmas trees surrounded by impressive TOK character depictions, all of them wearing Santa hats and elf shoes as they hang lights and decorate the trees.

I nudge Presley softly. "We're here."

"Mmmm," she murmurs, blinking a few times and then opening her eyes. Then they get wider, probably as she realizes she's leaning against me. She quickly straightens, still blinking sleep away. "Sorry about that," she says, gesturing toward my shoulder.

I wave her off, hoping that by acting normal, she'll feel normal too. "Like you said, I am taking up most of this seat. You didn't have a choice."

One side of her lips ticks up in a sleepy smile, and something swoops through my stomach.

What was that?

I quickly catalog what I ate this morning—a big breakfast burrito I made for myself last night to bring on the plane. (One for Presley too, of course.) All stuff I normally eat. Not that I really think that swoop had something to do with what I ate.

It's nerves for today, right?

Yeah.

She looks over at the bookstore, and her eyebrows jump. "Are you even going to fit in there?"

I chuckle. "Better chance at us being in the top twenty-five if no one else can fit in."

She pushes open her door, grabs her bag from the floor in front of her, and gets out. By the time I unfold myself from the vehicle, she's on the sidewalk in front of the store, stretching out and studying the storefront, her smile growing with every piece of the window art she takes in.

The crisp December air has a bite to it that's a little surprising since we came from California. But the day is sunny and looks like it will be beautiful. Plus I like the chill. It reminds me of home and the mountains around Little River. The air here definitely doesn't smell as clean, although there's a bakery down the street, and the scent of fresh bread drifts in the air. It's going to be a good day. I can feel it.

Presley gives a quiet squeal and claps her hands. "This is really happening!" Then she grabs my arm and tugs me toward the store. As she reaches the door, her cheeks go pink, and she drops my arm. Before she can say sorry again, I lean past her and open the door for her.

Both of our mouths drop at the noise level inside. There are at least fifty people in the store and it's over an hour before the sale officially begins.

Presley goes in first, taking in the scene with a look of awe. Maybe the estimate that there are around a hundred fans of this series is vastly under counted. There's always the chance that there are people out there reading the books and not getting involved with the forums and the fan page.

Then Presley's face falls as she takes in the number of people. "This is my fault," she says in a whisper-moan. "I thought for sure an hour would be plenty of time! There aren't that many fans."

I put an arm on her shoulder and shuffle her along the window to where I think the end of the line is.

"It's the bandwagon fans' fault," I correct her, scanning the crowd. Those nearest the front of the line look like hardcore fans. There's a lot of TOK merch being shown off—t-shirts, hoodies, bags, and other stuff with book art and quotes. Several people are reading books from the series as they wait. Plus I do recognize some of them from Facebook and the rare picture on the website forum. (You wouldn't be surprised at the number of profile pictures that are swords or the crest of Eldraeth.) But the people further back in the line lack any of these indicators. "I bet half these people don't even know about the TOK books," I say. "They just want in on the next big book thing."

A woman with long, sleek brown hair and no TOK merch on her person that I can see whips around to glare at me. And then the angry expression falls off her face just as quickly and is replaced with a flirty smile.

I ignore her and maneuver past a few more people. Sometimes being 6'7" and almost three hundred pounds helps you out. Sometimes it makes crowd situations awkward.

We finally find a spot in the back corner near an entire shelf dedicated to Sarah J. Maas. The swoop I previously noted in my stomach turns to a twist of discomfort when I see that Presley's eyes are shining a little as she surveys the bookstore, and not in a good way. She's pressing her lips together tightly, and then she turns away from me and sniffs into her hoodie like I won't notice.

I want to meet Thornridge, but Presley wants it so much more. My eyes find the woman with the dark hair again, and I notice at least a dozen more women like her, their outfits, hairstyles, and makeup, all screaming influencer rather than hardcore fantasy book lover. Several of them have phone stands set up and are taking carefully posed selfies—which would be fine, but none of them feature any of the TOK books. Not like the people here I can see are real TOK fans. Maybe it's the memory of Jett getting burned by an influencer like some of these women that makes me judge them so harshly, but I clench my jaw. Most of them won't get tickets to see Thornridge, so there's that. It doesn't make me feel better for Presley.

I shift so that I'm standing right in front of her, although she has her head turned like the display for a book called *A Court of Thorns and Roses* is fascinating to her.

"Pres?" I say softly.

She turns and looks at me. No tears have fallen yet, but her expression is utterly dejected. I hate hate hate that she feels this way.

She draws in a breath. "I thought I could ask him about Aunt Shannon. About how she got the book." She shrugs, like this is a small thing. That's the thing about Presley. Sure, she's not afraid to share stories about her aunt and shed tears over her when she talks to me, but she will also put on a smile and pretend like her grief is no big deal to make sure I'm not inconvenienced. I don't want her making herself small like that. Definitely not for me. I'm strong enough to hold her up when the grief makes her want to fall apart. Even over small things like finding out how her aunt got this book.

So you know what? I will burn this bookstore down to get her in the room with Thornridge if I have to. "Wait here," I say. "I'll be right back."

She furrows her eyebrows, but I move away before she can question me. With my height, I have the advantage of seeing that Sapphira Ranier, the bookstore owner, is standing near the front of the line in an animated conversation with a guy I recognize who runs the Facebook fan page and another woman. With so many people crowded around in this tiny place, getting to the front isn't easy.

"Excuse me," I say in my most polite voice when I reach Ms. Ranier.

She whirls and almost falls backward when she has to crank her head up to meet my eyes. "Wait," she says, pointing at me. "You look familiar."

The reason pretty much no one knows about how much I love TOK is because my TOK world very rarely crosses into my football world. Actually, meeting Presley was the first time it's happened, so the idea that Ms. Ranier might know who I am makes me raise my eyebrows. Although, she's probably just seen a meme somewhere. When I was a kid, dreaming of pro-football fame, having my face known because of memes was not what I pictured.

"Brock Hunter." I hold out my hand.

"Brock Bennet Hunter!" she repeats, adding in my middle

name, and her eyes brighten as she pumps my hand. "I recognize the name from the fan page." She grins widely. "You're very tall."

"Uh, thanks." My chest warms the slightest bit at her enthusiasm, and at not being recognized for throwing my helmet.

The crowd around us starts murmuring, and a few of the women I would've tagged as influencers have their phones out, either filming me or taking pictures. That's fine. That's what I need right now when I go into full celebrity mode. "I play football for the LA Rays … the, uh, pro-football team?" I continue when Ms. Ranier's gaze goes blank.

"Oh," she says. "A football player that loves TOK. I never would have thought. If I didn't know better, I'd have tagged you as a bandwagon fan, to be honest. We seem to have quite a few joining us today." I've only ever heard the term bandwagon fan used negatively, but Ms. Ranier says it cheerfully as she beams at the people crowding her bookstore.

"No. Not a bandwagon fan. I actually started reading TOK in middle school, and I've lost count of the number of times I've re-read it." These are not normally stats I announce to strangers, but this is a special situation. Also, I've never been embarrassed about my love of this book series; it's just not usually something other people care about.

"Really?" Ms. Ranier beams at me. "I love that. I'm so glad you're here, Brock!"

Her announcing my name seems to have confirmed my identity for the handful of people who know who I am. Several shouts of, "Brock, can I get a picture?" or "Brock! Over here! Can you sign my book?" start chorusing through the room. Ms. Ranier's eyes widen again.

Perfect. Usually when people are clamoring for me to talk to them or answer them or whatever, it's not a good thing for me, but this is all playing right into my hands. At least the fact that more people than usual know my name right now, thanks to the

Devils letting me go, is helping me right now. Silver lining, I guess.

"Ms. Ranier, can I talk to you for a minute?" I gesture to the one place in this store that isn't occupied—a small office that's the size of a broom closet. Fitting for a fantasy bookstore, if you ask me.

"Oh, call me Sapphira," she says. "What can I help you with?" She has to raise her voice over the din that's gotten louder as people still call for me and news seems to spread about who I am, probably along with explanations about why anyone should care.

"Please?" I gesture to the closet office again, and she finally nods and leads the way.

Here's the problem. I don't fit.

She steps inside first, and when I try to follow her, I basically put us in what Lyra might tell Kael is a compromising situation. So instead, I step back and hover in the doorway, hoping my voice doesn't carry. Or that the conversations will keep happening around the room to cover what I'm about to ask. I glance over my shoulder at Presley, and she's watching us with her head tilted in curiosity.

"What are you doing?" she mouths at me.

I give her a thumbs up and turn to Sapphira. "Listen, I will participate in whatever social media videos or commercials or whatever for TOK stuff you want if you can get me and my friend, Presley, into the gathering with Thornridge."

She immediately shakes her head. "I'm not in charge of that, Mr. Hunter—"

I flash my most charming smile. "You can call me Brock." Yeah, I have a reputation for putting my foot in my mouth with the media from time to time, but all those times I *didn't* say what I was thinking? That takes some major acting chops too. I'm telling you. And I will pull out every stop necessary to get this for Presley.

Sapphira lets out half of a breathy laugh before she cuts it off.

"Brock ... I'm sorry, but there's nothing I can do. I don't even have the tickets."

"Who has them?" I ask.

Sapphira pauses and then motions for me to step out of the doorway. She leans out, her hand on my arm, and I don't say anything about her familiarity. Sapphira Ranier is probably about fifteen years older than me, but I'll flirt with everyone in this room to get those tickets for Presley.

"Alexis?" she calls out. A woman at the sales counter looks up from an iPad. Sapphira waves her over.

"Brock," Sapphira says when Alexis reaches us. "This is Alexis Sterling, Mr. Thornridge's agent."

"Brock Hunter." I stick out my hand.

"He plays for the LA Rays," Sapphira says, but she ends it like a question, and I have to stop myself from laughing.

"The football team?" Alexis asks, shaking my hand and then dropping it. She's probably in her mid-fifties, but her look is very New York City power agent. Sleek, silver-gray hair cut in a short bob and impeccable makeup. I nod.

She taps a finger against her chin. "I've heard your name in the news."

I keep calm and try not to let my frustration show. "I just got traded to the Rays, so it's been around."

"I see. What can I do for you?" she asks.

"Tell her what you told me," Sapphira says encouragingly, so I repeat my request that Presley and I get to see Thornridge.

Alexis glances over her shoulder at the people still gathering. Twenty more people have squeezed into the shop since I arrived. "I *have* been pitching TOK to Hollywood," she muses. "Response hasn't been what I want, but if we can get even more buzz with someone like you talking about it—"

"I know Sophie Edwards and Layla Delaford," I break in. Again, I'll name drop every person in LA I can claim any kind of acquaintance with. "And Nick Cane," I add, remembering that Lincoln's dad is best friends with a TV network executive in LA.

Alexis's expression doesn't change from contemplative, but something flits through her eyes. She reminds me of my agent, with her cool, calm expression no matter the situation. She never even batted an eye when the Devils let me go, just went to work.

"I'll see what I can do," Alexis says. Then she turns and walks away.

That's not the answer I wanted, but there's also no way she's going to turn down my connections if she really is fishing for Hollywood on this. I make my way back to Presley. It's much harder than when I left since the store is filling up steadily. This has to be breaking the fire code.

"What was that?" Presley asks when I return to her side.

"Me playing the part of the diva most people think I am anyway."

She cocks her head to one side at the word diva, but then grabs my arm. "Did you get us in to see Thornridge?"

I grin at her. "I think so."

"Brock!" she whisper-shouts and shakes my arm. "That's not fair."

I lean toward her. "I don't care."

Her cheeks turn pink, and that's when I remember myself. Still, I don't want to ruin the ease we've had so I wait a beat before I step back and then pretend not to notice how long it takes her to remove her hand from my arm.

"Brock?" a voice calls to us from somewhere behind me. I turn to see the dark-haired woman I noted when we first walked in, pushing her way through the crowd toward us. "Hi, Brock!" She waves around a copy of *The Obsidian Kingdom,* the first book. It's pristine, and I'd bet money she bought it today.

She scowls at someone near her who presses against her and then she takes the final step toward us. She holds out the book. "Would you mind signing my book for me?" She holds a Sharpie in her other hand.

Gideon Thornridge would certainly hate this if he knew, but a glance at the front of the store shows Alexis's eyes on me. I need to show her my worth if she's going to help me get Presley in to see Thornridge.

"Sure," I say with a grin. I hold the book on top of a book shelf, pick a page that contains an important scene, and sign my name big across it. Hopefully if this woman gets a ticket, Thornridge won't notice my signature there.

"Thanks." She smiles widely at me. Her gaze turns to Presley, and the woman says, "Is this your girlfriend?"

"No," Presley says immediately and adds a fake, "Ha, ha, ha. No, definitely not his girlfriend."

Something pricks in my stomach, like her quick denial hurt my feelings. Which is stupid because I know exactly why she said something so quickly—she said she liked me last week, and I turned her down. Then she begged me to be friends again and promised it wouldn't be weird. She's making sure I know she's not going to harbor some unrequited crush.

Only, I don't like it.

Today is such a weird day. Maybe there *was* something in that burrito. I need to get a personal chef.

"I'm Presley." She gives the woman a small wave. "Brock and I are friends. We bonded over the TOK books."

"Oh, yeah?" the woman says. "So you're a booktoker too?"

That seems like it might be a shot at me and what I said when we came in the store. Still, I keep a smile on my face. It would not do for me to get let go from another team because I got into it with a woman in a bookstore over a fantasy series that's so obscure not even Hermione Granger's read it.

"Uh, no," Presley says. "TOK is what fans call The Obsidian Kingdom series. T-O-K."

The woman flushes, and I want to high-five Presley. She said it so sweetly, but she took this woman fully down a notch and labeled her as exactly what she didn't like me saying about her.

"Of course," she says. "I'm Bella Reese." She turns back to me. "It's so great to meet you."

I'm not sure what else to say.

She steps closer, waving her book around. "So you're a big fan?" She seems to have forgotten that Presley exists, turning fully to face me. Probably because of Presley's burn, even if she didn't mean it to be.

"Yeah." I nod toward Presley. "We both read it as kids. How about you?"

She doesn't acknowledge that I try to keep Presley in the conversation. "I love *anything* romantasy, so when I heard about it, I had to read it right away."

Romantasy? What does that mean? "Cool."

Bella puts a hand on my arm. "What did you think of ACOTAR?"

"ACOTAR?" I look at Presley.

"*A Court of Thorns and Roses*." She jabs a thumb behind her to the display.

"Ahh." I shrug at Bella. "Haven't read it."

She squeezes my arm, where she's still holding on. "You have to. You'll *love* it."

"Hey, Brock Hunter?" a voice says from behind Bella. Her eyebrows furrow at the interruption to our conversation. A hand appears with a notebook. Then a skinny kid who's probably sixteen or seventeen squeezes between Bella and someone with their back to us.

"Can I get your autograph?" the teen asks.

Bella scowls at him but shifts out of the way. Or tries to. The line in here has gotten bigger, if it's possible, and we're backed into the spaces between the bookshelves. Which are also packed in here tightly. The kid's wearing a New York Empire shirt so at least he's a football fan.

"Sure," I say, taking the notebook. He holds out a pen to me and I grab it. "You like TOK?" I ask. I can't help but be curious about how much my worlds are intersecting right now.

He nods vigorously. "Yeah. Love it. My dad read it to us for bedtime stories when we were little, but I've read them all myself now."

My smile stretches. "Oh, yeah?" I glance down at Presley to see that she's staring at the kid with big emoji eyes. She's smitten, and it's adorable. "What's your favorite?" I ask him.

"*Curse of the Obsidian Flame*, book three." He answers automatically, and if there was ever any doubt about him being an actual TOK fan, it's completely gone.

"Ooooo!" Presley says from beside me. "That's the one where Lyra and Kael kiss for the first time. It's my favorite too."

For the second time, Presley has made another fan go completely red. The boy scrubs the back of his neck. "That's not why," he says quickly.

Presley pinches her lips together. "Of course not."

The boy waves at me with the notebook. "Thanks, bro." Then he holds out three fingers and presses them against his heart in the Eldraeth sign of brotherhood. I grin, giving the gesture back before he melts into the crowd.

"Oh, my goodness. He's the cutest," Presley breathes from beside me. She's in heaven, surrounded by fans of her favorite series, and after signing the notebook for that kid, so am I.

She tugs on my arm, standing on her tiptoes, indicating she wants to tell me something. I tilt my head toward her.

"Bella wants your number," she whispers.

I glance to where Bella is standing with an elbow on top of a bookshelf, looking bored. She meets my gaze and instantly brightens.

"Why didn't she ask?" I whisper back.

Presley huffs out a breath that sounds like a laugh. "She was flirting. Obviously."

Now I'm careful not to look at Bella again. "Flirting?" I ask skeptically. "She just talked about books."

Presley raises an eyebrow. "Chat with me after you've read *A Court of Thorns and Roses*, and we'll visit her intentions again."

"What is that supposed to mean?"

She smirks.

My phone dings, and I pull it out to see a text from Lincoln.

Lincoln: Hope you don't mind being outed.

He attaches a screenshot of a social media post. It's a picture of me talking to Sapphira and Alexis and is accompanied by a caption that says: *New Rays Left Tackle, Brock Hunter, is a fan of The Obsidian Kingdom series! No way! Girlfriend just sent this to me from where she's at some signing for the series.* I'm tagged in the post, so I log in to Instagram to check it out. My heart sinks when I notice dozens of comments talking about how they're near enough to check this out. There are also plenty of comments saying how much they love that a football player isn't shy about reading some weird fantasy novel or showing up to be a super fan. But it also explains why there are a lot more people in this bookstore than Sapphira and Alexis probably planned. And as I look around, I notice that there are far more people here with t-shirts from various teams across the league—mostly New York Empire merch but a few Devils t-shirts and even a Rays one.

Presley suddenly slams into my side, and someone nearby says, "Oh, sorry." But people still push in. I've been zoned out while I look at the Instagram photo, but people are calling out my name, plenty who can't get near me because we're packed like sardines in here.

I quickly slip an arm around Presley. "You okay?"

"I'm fine," she chirps from where her face is now pressed into my ribs. She giggles.

"This is insane, Pres," I mutter.

She laughs again. "Says the guy who attracted half the people here. At least. Maybe most."

I huff in annoyance. This was supposed to be a day for me and Presley to celebrate our favorite book series finally getting completed. It's not turning out how I thought. "I'm a left tackle. This makes no sense. The only time people care about me is when I throw a tantrum and it makes a good meme."

"You're also a pro-football player, and I think that people

who aren't around them all the time think that's cool. I wouldn't know." She winks at me in a dorky way, making me laugh.

"Brock!" a woman shouts, pushing through the crowd and earning a lot of scowls and swear words, which she doesn't seem to care about. "Can you sign my jersey?"

It's my old one, from the Devils, and she points to her chest with one hand while waving a Sharpie at me with the other. She elbows someone aside to get closer, and it starts a domino effect. Before I can blink, Presley gets shoved to the floor with a cry of surprise.

I react instantly, scooping an arm under her back and hauling her up into my arms. No way is she getting trampled in this madness. I hold her close against me, my heart pumping fast with fear at how close she came to getting seriously hurt. Despite that scare, people are still jostling around me.

Instinct takes over. I swing Presley's legs up into my arms. "Make a path," I demand, and like Moses parting the Red Sea, it's done.

CHAPTER 18
PRESLEY

Brock holds me tightly against his chest like I'm a doll, and it means nothing to him. I've read about this in books. Kael does this in book three just pages before he and Lyra kiss for the first time. It's insanely romantic on the page, reading about the way she wraps her arms around his neck as he runs them to safety. Brock may not be running with me, but I have no doubt he could.

And basically, I will never be able to just be friends with him. He probably won't believe me that I could after today, too, because for the few minutes it takes him to carry me outside the bookstore to the sidewalk, I rest my face in the crook of his neck and breathe him in.

Falling with this crowd around me was scary, but it only lasted an instant before Brock had me protectively in his arms. Any fear from that has long since fled as he marches out with people still clamoring for him to sign something for them. Even the people at the front of the line that I was pretty sure were hard-core fans are begging now.

When we get outside, Brock stands next to the door. He lets out a long breath. The biggest thing is that he doesn't put me down. How long do I let this go before it makes things worse for our friendship? If I don't say anything, I can enjoy the way it feels to be held protectively in his arms and relish in a few daydreams. The problem is that it might prove to him that I can't be just his friend, and he would put a stop to us hanging out. If I keep our friendship, at least I can see him. It's a painful decision, considering how much I want to stay in his arms, but I have to make it.

"Um, Brock?" I tilt my head back to catch his gaze.

He looks down at me, his eyes still bright with the fear that took hold when he saw me down on the ground. His eyes rake over every part of my face, cataloguing me in a way that has warmth racing through me, head to toe. My mind goes to the scene with Kael and Lyra, how when she slid from his hold, he gripped her arms, pulled her back to him and crashed his lips to hers in a desperate way after fearing that he'd lose her.

It would be so easy to put my hand to Brock's cheek right now, guide his face toward me, kiss him again. It's so tempting even when I know how it ends.

"Presley, are you okay?" he asks. I can almost hear that note of desperation that the audiobook narrator put in Kael's voice when he asked the same thing before he kissed Lyra. Involuntarily, the sound makes my hands clench on his t-shirt, wanting it to be more than just a friend's concern. Brock is so loyal. He would have protected Lincoln or Layla the same way.

Reluctantly I say, "You can put me down now."

Pink tinges his cheeks. "Oh, right." He slips his hand from underneath my legs, gently setting me down on the sidewalk. The air feels cool on my neck, and I hope it means I'm not blushing too much. Or that Brock can explain away the red in my cheeks to the winter day. Other people spill out of the bookstore around us, the crowd milling near the door. Brock stands wide, making sure we have plenty of space.

"Thanks for saving me," I say, smiling up at him.

He stares at me for a long moment without answering. His

expression is confused, which I don't understand. Finally he shakes his head. "Yeah. It was my fault anyway."

Someone taps Brock's shoulder, asking for an autograph. He holds up a finger. "In a minute." He leans down over me, his face so close to mine I could turn and kiss him.

Why can't I stop thinking about kissing this man?

"I need to play nice with these people," he says quietly. "Are you really okay?" His voice sends shivers up my spine. It's low and protective. Put some armor on this guy, and he's my personal Sir Kael.

"I'm good. Really." I resist gripping his arms to keep him close to me.

As he pulls away, a voice from inside, the silver-haired woman that would make an excellent Elysande, calls for everyone's attention. She's one of the women Brock was talking to before. Everyone outside turns toward her.

"It's ten minutes early, but we have a much fuller house than expected," she says, and the statement is met with cheers. "Sapphira will pass out the tickets to the first twenty-five people who arrived." There's a collective groan through those who won't get them, and I let out a sad sigh myself. I don't see how Brock took care of this. Maybe he is Brock Hunter, and that means something in the football world, but here he's just another fan. Most of the people, besides that cool kid who loves the same TOK book I do, came to see Brock, not celebrate the release.

"I know," the woman says, holding up her hands. "We're so grateful for this support. So I have a surprise." Another cheer interrupts her, and when she waves her hands for quiet, the response is immediate.

"We're drawing *one* extra name randomly from the crowd to meet with Mr. Thornridge this afternoon. Sapphira is posting a link on the Obsidian Kingdom fan page on Facebook."

Brock and I share a knowing look. Half the bandwagon fans here will have a hard time finding it.

"Go there now and enter your name. We'll draw in about ten minutes, so hurry please."

Hope jumps through me. I still have a chance. I pull out my phone and look up at Brock, who's done the same. Only about half the people around us are looking at theirs, confirming my suspicions about a big chunk of this crowd. Brock grins triumphantly.

He leans over me again. "We've got this in the bag," he whispers, his eyes twinkling.

"I hope so." I click on the link, fingers shaking as I type my name in.

He nudges me with his elbow, softly. He's always so soft any time he touches me. Which, until that debacle inside the store happened, hadn't been a lot today.

"Trust me," he says.

I hit submit on the form and then turn to face Brock. "What *were* you talking to those two women about?"

He grins wider.

People continue coming up to Brock in the few minutes we have to wait for the announcement about who's getting the extra ticket. He hovers close to me, his arm brushing mine every so often as he reaches for a book or paper and a couple jerseys in some cases to sign for fans. I want to lean in every time, and *not* because he's warm despite the cold day. We were on such strange footing this morning—no longer the comfy, close friends we were before I admitted my feelings. Both of us trying hard to be that and failing because my admission is a big fat elephant in the room that's hard to get around.

And then the mayhem happened inside the tiny bookstore, and Brock went a little bit caveman, picking me up and hauling me to safety. The way he stared at me once we were out, checking over every inch of me—something changed again, and I don't know what to make of it.

Is it possible Brock feels the same way about me as I do about him … and he doesn't realize it?

I shake the thought away. It's silly, and probably my heart's way to grasp at straws and hope. Except for how he was clueless that the Booktok influencer was flirting with him. How she asked if I was his girlfriend? Classic. Could he have been clueless about my crush before and needs some time to catch up? It's too much to hope for, but I can't help myself.

"Okay, everyone!" The bookstore owner, Sapphira, claps her hands. "It's time to announce our special winner. Once we've done that, sales for *Veil of the Queen* will officially begin. You can purchase a copy up front, here"—she points to the counter and the iPad—"along with any other books you wish to purchase today. And of course, we will be handing out tickets to the first twenty-five people." She turns to look at the other woman, handing her a piece of paper. "Alexis? Would you like to do the honors?" Sapphira's eyes twinkle and she looks out the open door to Brock, then her gaze slides to me.

My heart jumps, and I turn to Brock, but he's leaning against the door frame opposite me all cool and casual. He grins at me again and my heart does another thump.

The sensible thing right now would be to cut off my friendship with Brock, even if it means losing the first person since Aunt Shannon to get me and my love for TOK. I can't just be his friend, and every moment that I stand here, knowing I won't ever be anything more to him, is pure torture.

But I can't walk away. The idea of not being around him twists in my stomach. I would rather have these bits and pieces for as long as I can and deal with the hurt later than give him up now.

"The winner …" Alexis says, holding up the paper with pomp. "Is Presley Tatum and a guest, if she would like."

"Yes!" I look to Brock and don't think twice before throwing myself into his arms. Almost as quickly, I realize I should pull away, but his arms tighten around my waist, and he lifts me up.

"Told you to trust me," he murmurs into my hair.

When he sets me back down, I give him the eye, but I can't

ask him outright what he set up with those women. They've clearly framed it as me being the spontaneous winner of a contest. I have no desire to cause a riot in this tiny bookstore.

Unless I end up in Brock's arms again …

"Thank you," I say quietly. I put my hands on his arms and squeeze, knowing that going in for another hug would be pressing my luck.

Brock just smirks.

CHAPTER 19
PRESLEY

Once we have our brand-new copies of *Veil of the Queen* in hand, and my tickets for the gathering with Gideon Thornridge, Sapphira instructs us to return to the bookstore at four p.m. to meet the author. "There's a meeting room in the back," she says, pointing to a door.

We don't have time to leave the area and sightsee in New York City, so we wander around the neighborhood and find some lunch. We have to take our food to a nearby park because Brock is so huge the tiny spaces in the restaurants can't accommodate him without them taking away tables nearby us. The temperature is in the forties, so not exactly warm. Brock acts like forty-five is shorts and t-shirts weather, and then hands me his jacket.

I hold out a hand. "Despite your claim, this is *not* t-shirt weather." I point to his thin t-shirt and then gesture to the park around us, the trees decked out in Christmas lights and wreathes with red bows hanging from lamp posts. "It's *Christmastime.*"

Brock takes one of my hands and puts it on his bicep. "Do I feel cold to you?"

I swallow. "No," I squeak. His muscles are impressive. This isn't new to me. The fact that his bicep is the size of my thigh is something I've noticed before, but having my fingers on his warm skin, feeling the breadth of his arm—yes, Lyra, I see you. I'm feeling a bit swoony.

Brock takes the jacket and drapes it over me, on top of the hoodie and jacket I'm wearing. The smell of his deodorant, something musky with pine in it, envelops me. I will never be the same again.

"So. Tell me how you got the ticket," I ask him, hoping he won't notice how disoriented he's made me by giving me his jacket. (And the bicep. That played a part too.)

He explains about the deal he made with Alexis Sterling, Gideon Thornridge's agent, and my mouth falls open. "You agreed to do anything on social media or an ad campaign? Brock. That wasn't smart. Let me give the ticket back."

"No way," he says immediately. "This is important to you. You want to see if he remembers signing the book for your aunt." He holds up a hand when I start to protest. "It's a win-win for me. Loving some obscure fantasy series and looking like a nerd? It's great for my rep. The media can't just see me as the angry guy who can't keep his mouth shut. If this is all over the internet, the fans, the commentators, everyone has to admit there's more than the clips that pop up when a team gets rid of me."

"Okay." I set down the slice of pizza I'm eating. "But that agent could hold you to anything now ..."

He waves his hand. "She looks like a shark, and I have no doubt she gets what she wants when she needs to, but she's been representing Thornridge for years and just now got him to finish the last book? And why would she be representing a series that barely got off the ground unless it's because she loves them too. She's a softie—I'm willing to bet on it."

I study him for a long moment, guilt that he offered up something so valuable to him—his reputation—all for me. "Lincoln says it's all over social media that you're a TOK fan."

He chuckles. "I know. My social media manager has been

texting me all afternoon. She says to warn her next time I pull something like this. But she's loving it."

"Lincoln says *everyone* is loving it."

Brock finishes off his pizza slice. "Told you," he says with a shrug.

I let it go. Maybe later I'll push Brock to examine what he did for me today and what it means, but I still doubt that he has feelings for me. His actions today could be out of loyalty to our friendship. I'm not going to put myself out there again only to be embarrassed again. I need to be sure.

I can't wait any longer to open *Veil of the Queen*. I pause for a moment to admire the shiny cover again. I've done that a couple times since we left the bookstore with our books in brown gift bags with The Sorcery Shop printed on them. Our tickets are tucked safely in my bag.

Lyra is depicted front and center of the cover, in an elaborate gown of shimmering gray and silver. She has a cloak that is swept out behind her and the hood hides most of her face, only her determined eyes peeking from behind its shadows. Kael is the second most prominent figure, standing behind her, decked out in his armor, hand on the hilt of his sword, and looking sexy with his long hair pulled back from his face.

This book has to be around a thousand pages long. Goosebumps rise up along my skin as I contemplate reading it. A new TOK adventure. I'll get to read about Lyra and Kael and all the other characters for the first time again. It's been so many years since I did that, over ten since I read book fifteen for the first time when it came out when I was in high school.

"It's almost like a reverent moment, starting this one, isn't it?" Brock says in a soft voice.

"Exactly." My voice is a whisper. He feels like the only person in the world that gets it. So how can he not be *my* person?

I carefully lift the cover, studying the title page first. Even the title art is drawn beautifully, and I run my fingers over it. Brock leans toward me, and I turn the book so we can both admire it. If he moves over to my side of the picnic table, we'll likely tip it over.

The dedication is to Thornridge's "patient fans," which Brock and I both chuckle over.

"If you're going to start reading this right now, you have to read aloud," Brock says.

"I don't think I want to start if I can't spend a significant amount of time reading." I stare at the first page, the words bleeding in even though I try hard not to let them.

Brock's voice startles me. "'The winds whispered of change, carrying with them the echoes of long-buried secrets, as the Obsidian Kingdom prepared for its reckoning.'"

I have to swallow back the words, *If you don't want me to fall in love with you, don't ever do something like that again.* I'm stunned into silence by how utterly sexy it is hearing him read to me. It conjures an image of him relaxing on my couch, like the night we watched a Christmas movie together, but with me leaning against his chest. I would have my TV playing one of those fireplace videos, because of course. He's holding *Veil of the Queen,* in one hand, which he can do because his hands are so massive, and his other is around me, his fingers playing with the ends of my hair.

My insides ignite.

"Presley?" Brock says, yanking me from the delicious daydream.

"Hmm?" I try my best to look innocent, but I'm pretty sure I was staring at him.

"You were staring at me …" he says. Okay, that confirms it.

"Uh, zoned out while you were reading. Have you ever considered being an audiobook narrator? I think you'd be good." The words come out in a rush.

"Maybe once the football thing is over."

"Good plan." Or maybe I can convince him to read just for me. That's totally a friends thing, right?

I look down at my watch to avoid eye contact with Brock. I'm afraid of what's written in my face, and if he sees too much, he might run away from me again. This whole day is dangerous for the state of our friendship, and I should have known that. "Should we head back over early?" I suggest. "Just so we don't repeat this morning's fiasco. I mean, we have tickets, but now that word is out that Brock Hunter loves TOK, there could be a riot."

He scoffs, but his expression is amused. "Good idea."

We gather up our lunch garbage and head back to the bookstore. I give Brock back his jacket once we're walking and I warm up. Besides, I have to pretend it was about warmth and not … more. I'm grateful for the brisk air against my face hopefully chasing away any heat that lingered after my silly daydream. I need it to clear away my thoughts. They aren't helping anything.

Unless I'm right about him not recognizing his feelings.

I mentally bat that away too. Not helpful right now.

There is a crowd at the bookstore but mostly outside. A man stands at the door, and he would probably look beefier if I wasn't standing next to a pro-football lineman. This man is a few inches taller than me, almost six-foot maybe, but stocky and muscled.

"Are you here to buy books?" he asks. "Or to stalk Brock Hunter?"

Brock covers laughter with a cough, but not quickly enough. The guy looks up at him and raises an eyebrow. And yet … no recognition.

So I say it. "Well, this *is* Brock Hunter, and we're here for the meet and greet with Mr. Thornridge." I show him the tickets from my bag.

The man's face breaks into a grin. "Come on in. Sorry, Mr. Hunter. I'm a soccer fan, to be honest. Never watch football. Sapphira is my sister and called me because you all had a little trouble this morning. You looked like a football fan." He shrugs, clearly unbothered by not recognizing Brock.

"Good call," Brock says, holding out his knuckles for a fist bump. "I *am* a pretty big football fan." They both laugh, and the man motions for us to enter the shop.

Unlike this morning, only a few customers mill around, and they're actually browsing books. A woman looks up when we enter and glares at us. I'd bet money she's one of the actual TOK fans that didn't end up with a ticket this morning. Brock nods at her, and I force a smile, but her glare only deepens, and she goes back to reading *Veil of the Queen* as she leans against a bookcase.

Sapphira makes a show of checking our tickets at the door, which is obviously unnecessary except for Cranky Lady hovering nearby. By my quick headcount, the other twenty-five ticket recipients are already here. Folding chairs are set up in the small room and there's a folding table at the front stacked with copies of the other books in the TOK series.

Brock and I take seats in the back. There are only three left in the corner, but it wouldn't have mattered. Brock couldn't have crammed himself into one of the rows closer to the front even if I wanted him to. Everyone else is seated, chatting amongst themselves. There are still thirty minutes before Thornridge is scheduled to come. Brock scoots along the back wall, and I follow him to the remaining open seats. He pulls one away from the row, setting it closer to the wall before sitting carefully in it. We share a relieved glance when it doesn't buckle out from underneath him, and then we grin at each other.

"Let's make it a point to bring our own, reinforced chairs next time we come to one of these," I say.

"Agreed."

I pull out *Veil of the Queen* again.

"Are you going to read that out loud to me?" Brock asks pointedly.

"You have a copy." I gesture to the brown gift bag at his feet.

He puts his hand on my book, preventing me from opening it. "This is the last time we'll get to read a TOK book for the first time. We should … we should read it together."

I tilt my head at him. I love that he wants to share this with me. "We will." I wink at him. "I'm just going to beat you, obviously."

He keeps his hand covering the book and stares at me earnestly. "No. I mean together. Reading it aloud to each other. Really experiencing it *together*."

I draw in a quick breath. I couldn't tell him no even if I wanted to. "That might take a long time," I say cautiously. What I don't say is that I could ruin our friendship again by then. How will I keep things friendly between us when he's reading a book to me in the sweet, sexy voice of his? How will I not jump in his lap and kiss him when Thornridge reunites Lyra and Kael after they've been apart for almost two years? (He better reunite them.)

"I've never had someone like you in my life, Pres. Someone to really share this with. I want to make it memorable because this is it."

I'm nodding before he even finishes talking. "Okay."

"Okay?"

I keep the book in my lap, but I don't open it while we wait. Instead we talk about football, and Brock jokes about how tired he's going to be tomorrow. I beam at him when he promises me that it's totally worth it. I tell him about how I got the job as a physical therapist with the Rays thanks to my dad and then we talk about my dad for a while since Brock knows about him. He seems to enjoy it when I relay how he and his friend Jeff reassured me that Brock would definitely get signed somewhere.

Before we know it, Sapphira calls for everyone's attention and announces Gideon Thornridge. He appears through a side door at the front of the room, waving cheerfully to everyone as he comes to take a seat at the table amid wild clapping for so small a crowd. Alexis follows him inside, taking her place at his side. She gives a nervous glance around the room and then her shoulders relax, probably when she confirms that it's only true TOK fans here, not rowdy Brock Hunter fans. She smiles when her gaze turns to our corner of the room, and Brock returns the expression.

Gideon Thornridge looks just like his picture in the backs of the books, though obviously older. His wavy hair, which is tousled and stands straight up—and not in a fashionable way— is threaded through with gray. His thick-rimmed glasses hide some of the lines around his eyes. His smile is wide. He's tall and lanky, something I couldn't have gotten from a picture, but it doesn't surprise me.

"Hello, everyone," he says, and various greetings echo back to him.

"We're going to do a fifteen-minute question-and-answer session," Alexis says officially, "and then you can line up to have Mr. Thornridge sign your books."

"No mister, here, Alexis," Mr. Thornridge says, waving a hand at his agent. "Just Gideon. Everyone here is a good friend." He beams. I like him so much.

I can barely focus during the question-and-answer portion. I keep thinking about what I'm going to say and pulling up the picture of Aunt Shannon that I put in my phone's photo's favorites folder to make sure it was easily accessible.

Someone asks if Lyra is the Obsidian Queen, and Gideon chuckles and says, "Next," making everyone else laugh. Someone else asks what took so long for this book. The answer is surprising enough that I pay attention while he's talking.

"It's been written for about ten years, to be honest. I was waiting until the time felt right." He leaves it at that, even though everyone murmurs, and the next question is, "Why is now the right time?" He waves it off and says in that same calm tone, "Next."

I bounce my foot through questions about who the characters are based off of and if there are going to be more. ("Definitely not," he says to that.) Questions about if he's going to write more books, and he shrugs at that too.

Brock puts his hand on my leg to still it, and everything else fades as I look over at him. He doesn't meet my gaze, just rests his hand on my thigh. He gives it one small squeeze and leaves his hand there.

I *know* it's about comfort and calming, but my leg is on fire. My entire body is on fire. I don't calm down like Brock intended because my thoughts are racing around him. Aching for him. Wanting to scoot my chair closer and snuggle up against his side while we listen to Gideon.

The question-and-answer session goes past fifteen minutes, and Alexis finally ends it and invites people to come forward to have their books signed.

"Calmly," she says firmly, eyeing the crowd. Brock presses his lips together, his expression amused. "Mr. Thornridge is only signing *Veil of the Queen* and one additional book for time's sake. You are welcome to chat with him for a few minutes, but I will be limiting the time so that everyone has an opportunity. Thank you so much for coming."

Brock stands first and takes my hand in his, pulling me forward quickly. There's murmuring in our wake, but no one's going to challenge him. There's one guy in here who's almost as tall as him, maybe six-four, but he's still at least half Brock's size. We end up fifth in line to talk to Gideon.

My hand is shaking, and I don't know if it's because I'm nervous or because Brock is still holding my other one. It's not romantic. His hand engulfs mine. It must feel like a child's hand to him the way he's wrapped it around mine—no fingers tangled together. That's probably why he hasn't noticed that it *doesn't feel like we're just friends right now.*

I remind myself that for Brock, this is all about getting me my moment to talk to Gideon, to ask him about my aunt. It's about friendship and taking advantage of who he is to get favors called in. This is all stuff he'd do for Lincoln or Layla.

It's nothing special, and I tell myself that for the twenty minutes we wait for it to be our turn.

Gideon looks at Brock when we reach the front, a grin splitting his face, but Brock nudges me forward gently with a hand on my back. Gideon gives Brock one more glance then turns his attention to me, still smiling.

I set down my new copy of *Veil of the Queen* on the table. "Hi, my name is Presley Tatum. It's really cool to meet you." I want to slap my forehead for sounding like a fourteen-year-old at a One Direction concert, but I just keep my smile plastered on.

"Ah, Miss Tatum," he says like he knows me. Does he frequent the forums? He'd see my name there often enough. My hopes that he'll remember Aunt Shannon raise. "Are you ready for this?" he asks, handing the book back when he's signed it.

I draw in a breath. Given that I just said I'd read it out loud with Brock, probably not. "I've been waiting a long time," I say instead. A year ago, if I'd had this chance to meet Gideon Thornridge like this, conversation with him would have been easy, even the small talk. But the only thing I can think of is Aunt Shannon and that mysterious signature. I reach inside my bag and pull out the collector's edition of *Rebirth of Darkness*.

His eyes light up as he takes it in his hands. "Yes, a true fan indeed to have this edition. Do you have all fifteen?"

"Of course."

He moves to open it, and I hurry to speak. "It's actually already signed," I say in a rush. He arches a brow, and words tumble around in my head but none come out. I swallow. How will I talk about Aunt Shannon without falling apart? Then Brock's hand moves lightly across my back, and he slips it around my waist, cupping it there in a comforting way. Everything inside me settles. Whatever this is between us, Brock *is* my person.

"My aunt left that for me when she … uh, passed away a year ago. But I don't know how she got it signed. She never told me, and I didn't know she'd done it until it was too late to ask. I was hoping you'd remember." *Praying* he'd remember. Banking on the fact that he signs so few books that something would stick with him about this book.

He opens the book in a reverent way, looking down at the writing there. After a moment he smiles sadly. "She passed?" he asks, looking up at me, his expression full of compassion, not curiosity.

I nod, unable to say anything else. Brock squeezes my side, and I take a deep breath, letting his touch settle me again. Maybe tomorrow we'll go back to dancing awkwardly around our relationship, but for now, this helps.

Gideon signals to Alexis, and she asks the people standing behind us in line to please take a few steps back. I lean in on instinct when he lowers his voice. "I also write romantic comedies, under a pen name," he says. I was not expecting to hear that. Beside me, Brock sucks in a startled gasp. "They are … quite a bit more lucrative than TOK," Gideon goes on. "TOK is my passion, but those books pay the bills." I can't help it; I let out a small breathy laugh. Aunt Shannon would have loved knowing that. "In one of my romcoms, there is a passing reference to Lyra and Kael. Your aunt found it, probably one of only a few people who would have even noticed it. That author persona is much more present online, and your aunt hunted me down and figured me out. In exchange for keeping my secret, I sent her this. That was about"—he looks at his watch—"just over a year ago."

I clamp my lips together to keep a hiccupping breath from escaping. It would have been weeks, maybe even days, before her accident. She probably planned on telling me all about it.

Gideon looks down at the signature again and then closes the book as reverently as he opened it. His eyes are shining when he hands it back to me. "Her personality showed through those emails. I'm more sorry than I can say to learn that you lost her." He gives a quiet chuckle. "She was very complimentary about my other books."

I have to read them. If Aunt Shannon loved them—if she found that small piece of TOK in them—I want to love them too. "Mr. Thornridge—"

"Gideon," he corrects.

"May I know your pen name?"

He looks around, and I hide my amused reaction to how secretive he is about the TOK faithful finding out about his other books. He reaches for a sticky note from a pile of things beside him—sharpies, bookmarks, even a few paperclips—and scribbles something on it and then hands it to me.

I read it and then look up at him, eyes wide. "You? Seriously?" At least three of his books are movies, one in theaters and two others on streaming platforms. I've heard two more are in the works. Everyone on Booktok has read these books. Bella the Booktoker would die if she knew.

He grins.

I tuck the sticky note into *Rebirth of Darkness* and close it, putting it in my bag and then giving him a solemn nod.

"A pleasure to meet you, Miss Tatum." He holds out his hand and I take it, shaking it. He holds on, patting my hand softly with his other before letting go.

"Thank you." I step aside since Alexis is getting shifty. She obviously picked up on the importance of our conversation and didn't interrupt, but we've gone over the few minutes of time she has allotted to each ticketholder.

Also, no wonder he has a shark for an agent. I pat *Rebirth of Darkness* again, thinking about the name he gave me. Impressive.

CHAPTER 20
BROCK

Gideon Thornridge's voice turns hearty and amused when I move to give him my copy of book sixteen to sign. "I've heard you caused a little bit of a ruckus today, Mr. Hunter."

Urban legend says this man stopped signing books because someone mistook him for J.R.R. Tolkein, so I grimace rather than laugh. It's probably that—a legend, given how he's acted with Presley and what he revealed to her. That revelation also makes me wonder why Alexis didn't just brush off my offerings to get Presley this ticket. They clearly already have all the connections she needs to get movies made.

"Sorry about that, sir."

He waves me off. "It was the delight of my day when Alexis called to report to me that Brock Hunter was a fan of TOK."

He says my name like he knows it. "You're a football fan?" I can't help asking. There's a middle-school boy in me still whose mind would be blown to discover that the author of TOK liked football.

"A casual fan," he says. "I watch an Empire game here and there. Brie Delaney had me up in her suite last year, and that was very enjoyable, to be honest."

I'm guessing Ms. Delaney, the owner of the Empire, is in on

the secret of Gideon's pen name. "If you ever want to watch a Rays game from a suite, let me know." I look up at Alexis, who made all of this happen for us today. "Same to you."

"I might hold you to that," she says.

"Are you ready for this?" Gideon asks the same thing he asked Presley as he opens *Rebirth of Darkness* to sign it.

"I've known for years what happens," I say with a wink at Presley, which draws a full chuckle from Gideon. She elbows me, shaking her head. She won't say it in front of Gideon, but if Lyra *is* the Obsidian Queen, she might burn every copy of the TOK series she owns. Except for the one her aunt gave her, maybe.

Gideon asks me how I found TOK, and we chat for a minute about Tim and his influence on my life before Alexis gives me a look that says I've gotten away with enough today.

"Thank you again for this opportunity," I say as a way of goodbye. I wave at Alexis too.

"One moment, Brock," Gideon says before I shift away. He holds out a notebook, and I notice the signature of a few A-list names in Hollywood on the page he's on before he turns to a new one. "May I have *your* autograph."

I can't help beaming at him. Yes, fourteen-year-old Brock's mind would be thoroughly blown at this moment. "Absolutely."

Presley and I don't speak until we're outside the little bookstore. The rest of the world seems like a surprise after that.

"Wow," she says, shaking her head. "I can't believe that happened. He's—" She cuts herself off before she says the name.

"He asked for my autograph." A disbelieving laugh escapes me.

"He's so cool." Presley hugs her bag to her chest.

"The coolest." The SUV I rented for us today idles at the curb, waiting for us to get in. I'd texted our driver when we got to the front of the line so we wouldn't have to wait too long. We need to grab dinner and get on the plane back to LA. I have to go to practice in the morning.

But I'm not quite ready to leave yet. Today has been magical, and being here with Presley is a huge part of that. I think about how compelled I was to make sure she got every single thing she deserved today and the warmth that climbed up my arm when I held her hand. The feeling that I would have traded myself back to the Devils if it meant that Presley could get the answers she wanted about her aunt. What does it mean that I didn't care if we got special treatment today just because I'm a rich football player who threw around my weight to get Presley what she wanted? I have a suspicion, but I push it away for now. Today has been perfect, and I don't want to ruin it.

"Selfie?" Presley asks.

"Obviously."

She hands me her phone, and we laugh as we try to adjust in the picture to get Presley's head in it along with the bookstore behind us.

"Do we need to get you a stool to stand on?" I ask.

"Maybe you should crouch, you giant."

So I do that, which makes her laugh harder, and that's when I snap the picture.

It's perfect.

We head back to Teterboro and find a little grill restaurant for dinner. We linger too long, reliving the best moments from the day. Presley's cheeks turn rosy when she talks about me carrying her to safety from my rabid fans. We both know we should hurry. We have to work in the morning, but I get the feeling Presley's holding on to today like I am, somehow knowing the magic is going to end.

Finally we head over to the airport, where our plane is waiting for us. It's nice flying a private jet, and worth every penny. Presley and I would have had to rush through everything without it. Despite the pressure I live with because of football, I'm grateful it provided us with this.

To be honest, everything in my life has felt easier to deal with since I met Presley, and that's not lost on me.

We settle onto the plane while it gets ready to leave, and I pull out my copy of the new TOK book. "Ready to start?" I ask.

"I've been waiting all day, Book Tsar." She reaches inside her bag.

I hold up a hand, stopping her. "Come over here and read to me. You're first." I took a seat on the love seat that's situated on one side of the plane since it accommodates my large stature a lot better. I point to the seat next to me. "So I can make sure you're reading it right and not skipping things you don't like."

Presley doesn't answer for a long moment, just studies me, eyes boring into mine. "Lyra *isn't* the Obsidian Queen," she finally says and steps across the aisle to plop down next to me. I take up a lot of room on any piece of furniture I sit on, but especially this one. It can't be true love-seat size since the space I've left for her puts her right next to me, her leg touching mine as she sits down.

I hand her the book, again pushing aside the warmth that creeps over my leg from where she's touching me. I'll think about that tomorrow. I stretch my arm across the top of the love seat. She turns to glance at it but then stares at the book.

"Not sure I'm ready for this," she says quietly as she stares down at it.

Oh, I know the feeling.

"Even when we finish this book, TOK doesn't have to end. We can read it together a dozen more times." I let my arm slip off the love seat and around her shoulders, pulling her in for a side hug.

"A dozen," she says, her soft voice scoffing. "Slow poke." She leans into my side and opens the book. I relax beside her.

In the early hours of the next morning, after I've walked Presley up to her apartment and hugged her goodnight, I text Lincoln as I make my way back down to the SUV.

Brock: I think I messed up.

CHAPTER 21
PRESLEY

Wednesday crawls by despite how busy I am catching up on the work I missed the day before. I should be more tired, considering I was so keyed up after Brock dropped me off that I didn't fall asleep until after three this morning. So much was running through my brain, specifically the fact that for at least half of the plane ride, *I cuddled with Brock while we read TOK.*

Just like my daydream.

He expects this to continue—me and him, sitting together and reading. He already plans on coming over tomorrow. No big reveals have happened in the book yet, but we're both eager to find out which of us is right about the Obsidian Queen. We'd read together tonight, but we also both agree we need to catch up on sleep.

I definitely need to, or I'm going to do something stupid like tell him my feelings for him again. Everything about yesterday felt so at odds with him saying that he didn't feel the same way about me that I did for him and him worrying about me getting the wrong idea from our friendship.

Is this what he means? That I would read into the hand-holding and the cuddling and the carrying me to safety stuff?

For goodness sake, what girl wouldn't?

I drive straight to my mom's after work. I have things to talk to her about. Getting her opinion on what kept Aunt Shannon from telling me about the book for one. Asking her what she thinks about the way Brock acted yesterday for another, although I suspect I know what she's going to say. She was so sure he liked me before. She's going to be positive now.

I don't know if that helps me.

I need to find more friends than just my mom.

Mrs. Westcott is marching up the street from her house when I pull up. I quickly duck down, although that probably makes me look guiltier than just facing her. I rise a little to peer out the window, relieved when she passes by my parents' house and goes on down the street. She's wearing flared leggings, walking shoes, a long sleeved shirt, and a vest along with a beanie. And her arms are moving in a classic power-walker way. She's exercising. Not out to interrogate. Still I wait for her to round the block before I venture out of my car. I could not hold it together if she stopped to talk with me. Not when I have her ring in my possession.

I have to figure out how to get it back to her without me ending up arrested in the process.

I take a deep breath, pushing thoughts of the ring out of my mind so Mom doesn't read them on my face, and head for the front door. "Hey!" I call after I've tapped in the code and push the door open.

My dad sits in one of the big recliners. He holds up a book. "I went to your house and got book five yesterday. Hope you don't mind."

I make my way into the living room. "You're the slowest reader I've ever met."

"I may be retired, but I'm not lying around the house all day reading."

I pick up a pillow from the couch and throw it at him.

"I thought once you left the house, my pillows would be

safe," Mom says, coming into the room. She walks right over to Dad, picks up the pillow, and puts it back.

I whirl on her. "I'm going to need your whole collection of those romcom books you and Aunt Shannon both loved." I head over to the floor-to-ceiling bookcases in the room, searching for the section where she keeps them. "Even the ones Aunt Shannon gave you."

"Which ones?" Mom walks over to join me, eyeing me while I search.

I throw out my hands, finally finding the name I'm looking for. "The ones that are apparently written by my favorite fantasy author." I start pulling them off the shelf. There are about five with double copies, one of Aunt Shannon's and one of Mom's. The reference Aunt Shannon found is probably in one of those. I'll google search for it later.

"What are you talking about?" Mom asks.

My pile is growing. I'm going to need something to carry them in. "Do you have a box or something?"

Mom puts a hand on my arm, stopping me from the mess I'm making. "You seem … full of energy, Pres. How did yesterday go?" Her eyes rake over my face with an expression unique to mothers—a mix of detective and therapist all in one, I think. She's searching for clues and readying herself for whatever emotions start spilling out.

"I don't even know." I throw up my hands. "But I don't want to talk about Brock yet."

Mom leans back from me, bewildered. "I didn't ask about Brock."

"Well." I huff and then take a deep breath. "You should, but not yet."

She blinks slowly at me. "Okay. So did Mr. Thornridge remember Shannon?"

"He did." Already tears sting my eyes. It sounds so like Aunt Shannon to stalk him like that. "I have the biggest secret to tell you, and you can't tell a soul. Aunt Shannon promised, and I'm pretty sure Gideon expects me—and you—to uphold that."

Mom holds up a hand as though she's testifying in court. "I promise."

"Gideon Thornridge has a pen name. One that he writes some very popular books under." I hold up one of the romcoms and tap the name pointedly.

Mom's eyes widen. "Are you serious?"

"As serious as the Forces of Vorath."

Dad snorts, but Mom frowns at me. "I don't know what that means."

I wave her away. "Aunt Shannon found a vague TOK reference in one of these books," I gesture to the mess I've made, "and figured it out. Then he sent her the signed book. I just don't know why she hadn't given it to me."

Mom squints at me, like she's trying to remember. "I'm sure she was going to. That book was on her nightstand after the funeral." Mom chews on her lip the way she does when she's going to cry and doesn't want to. "I didn't need a sticky note to know it was for you. I put it in your box, but I'm guessing she'd planned on showing it to you right away. And then …"

Neither of us needs her to finish that. Then she fell and hit her head and died years before ALS was supposed to take her. We knew she was going to die within ten years. She was already planning for it, but the way we lost her was worse, I think. Expecting more and being robbed of all of it.

We both stare down at the book in my hands. It's one that's about to be released as a movie on Netflix.

"So, about Brock?" Mom says slowly.

I lie back on the carpet and stare at the ceiling for several seconds before I answer. "Yesterday was … weird. But also amazing. I don't know what to think about it."

Mom turns so that her back is against the bookcase. "Weird good?"

"Yeah, but like in a 'just for today' kind of way. Well, that's what it felt like. We started out super awkward, both of us being careful about what everything meant, you know? Then things got crazy at the bookstore," I remind her. I texted her about it while we were waiting for Gideon to come to the signing because she'd seen some pictures on Instagram.

"He carried you outside." Mom smirks.

I cover my face with one hand. "And from there it was like friends with a few benefits the rest of the day. He held my hand—not romantically but still. And basically had me cuddle with him during the plane ride home."

"Hmmm." Mom studies me. "So he realized he was wrong about how he felt."

I throw up my hands toward the ceiling. "Or he doesn't realize how he feels at all. I don't know. I'm so confused."

"Talk to him."

I sit up and wag a finger at her. "No, no, no. Been there, not doing that again."

Her expression turns patient. "I'm not saying you need to say that you have feelings for him. I'm saying you can tell him that yesterday was confusing, and you'd like to know more about how he feels about it. Like grownups."

I let out something between a moan and a sigh. "So much easier said than done. I need him to admit something to me. I can't be chasing him around like some obsessed fan."

"Presley …"

I hold up a hand. "Mom. Pretend for five seconds that I'm not your perfect daughter that every man I come in contact with can't help but fall in love with—"

"If they all haven't, they should have their eyes checked," Dad interrupts from his recliner.

I wave a hand around in his direction. "Not helping. Mom, can you pretend like I'm a normal girl for a few minutes and be logical about this?"

"Definitely not." She shrugs.

I sigh. "Talking to him won't help if he doesn't realize what's going on. I just have to make him see it."

"Maybe suggest an appointment with the eye doctor," Dad says.

"Go back to your reading, old man. See if you can finish this series before you lose *your* sight."

He throws a pillow at me and immediately gets scolded by Mom. My parents are the best.

CHAPTER 22

BROCK

I texted Lincoln so early this morning that it's not surprising that he doesn't respond until I'm already on my way into the facility for practice.

"What does that mean?" My phone reads the text to me. "I've scoured social media. You didn't say anything stupid yesterday, and everything is about how you're so hot because you love some nerdy book series."

I don't bother responding. I'll talk to him at practice.

He's waiting for me when I come into the weight room at eight a.m. It feels a lot earlier, given the lack of sleep I got last night. Yesterday was all worth it, though. I'd do it all again for the joy in Presley's face.

"What did you mean?" Lincoln falls into step with me as I head to the rack to start my strength workout. There's worry in his eyes, but his expression looks like he's trying to stay calm.

"I messed up with Presley," I say to ease his mind on the football front.

If anything, his expression gets tighter. I don't blame him. Chelsi, the only other female trainer on staff, is already married. The guys have a protective big-brother vibe going on with Presley.

"I'm not going to jump to conclusions," he says, his tone level. "Hurry up and explain."

So I do. I tell him about how I realized I'd do anything to get Presley what she wanted, what it felt like to hold her in my arms, the warmth I felt holding her hand and when I put my hand on her knee. How I pulled her close on the plane to read the book with her.

By the time I'm finished, Lincoln is grinning from ear to ear. "So, you like her," he finishes for me.

"Yeah, and somehow I didn't see it until it was too late." Was it the fact that the way I felt crept up on me? That it happened so slowly I didn't realize it was there until she was in my arms and I was carrying her to safety? I don't want to over-dramatize that moment when she fell, but my fear that she could've been seriously hurt was real. It was like everything was pulled out of me for a moment, and when it all came rushing back in, it was obvious how I felt about her.

The stuff I was looking for—the way Kurtis spoils my mom, how Lincoln always wants to be around Layla, the way Tim can't keep his eyes off Meg—it was all there suddenly, but in the little things.

I do want to give Presley the world, but not the gifts like Kurtis does. I want to give her comfort with her grief over her Aunt Shannon when it rises up. I want to make her laugh with my silly theories about the books. Yesterday, I wanted to give her the answers she couldn't find on her own, and I was willing to be a fool on social media for her to do it.

And from the moment I held her in my arms, the way I've been orbiting around her since day one became evident. The texts I answer after my bedtime. The person I wanted to talk to when the Devils dropped me was her. When I thought our friendship was lost, it hurt.

I fell in love with Presley Tatum little by little and never saw it because I thought it had to look like everyone else's relationships.

"What do you mean 'too late'?" Lincoln's question pulls me out of my thoughts. He's waving Eli over, and Anthony Hurley follows in Eli's wake.

I should have foreseen where this confession would lead me. I only have myself to blame now. "Yeah," I reply. "I can't just tell her how I feel after I shut her down like I did. Plus she's a trainer for the team. I'm not sure that's even … ethical or whatever." I can't break rules, not when I just got here. But staying away from Presley also feels impossible.

Lincoln puts a hand on my shoulder. "That first part—that's stupid. The quickest way to get yourself out of this mess would be to tell her what you told me: that you messed up and you want a redo."

"And the second?" I ask the same time Eli joins us and says, "What's up?"

I don't know Eli Dash that well, but he's one of Lincoln's best friends, so I extend my trust in Lincoln to him.

Lincoln answers. "Hunter finally realized it."

I'm sure Eli is going to need more explanation than this, but he just grins at me. "Seriously, man. I was beginning to wonder."

I massage the bridge of my nose. "I don't understand how you all can be so sure about something I didn't even know myself."

"I told them about Natasha," Lincoln says.

"Also Faith," Eli points out.

Lincoln nods. "Right."

I fix Lincoln with a glare. "Seriously?"

"Please, tell me another way to explain you." He raises an eyebrow at me skeptically.

"Guys." I hold my hands out, addressing all three. "I'm very grateful for your support here"—I make sure they hear my sarcasm—"but none of this helps the fact that Presley is a trainer, and I cannot get caught breaking rules."

"It's not against the rules," Eli says. He folds his arms. He's several inches shorter than me, and I have at least thirty pounds on him, but he's a confident quarterback. He owns the stance.

"We asked Coach," Lincoln adds.

"You told Coach you thought I had feelings for Presley?" This is a line too far. It's one thing for him to team up with half the offense to do matchmaking, but telling coach?

"First, we *knew* you had feelings for Presley," Lincoln corrects.

Eli grins at me. "Also, we told him Hurley wanted to date Presley."

Hurley smirks and wags his eyebrows. I narrow my eyes at him, but it does nothing to wipe the expression off his face, only makes his eyes dance.

"Coach said it's not against the rules. They don't encourage personal relationships between the players and the training staff," Lincoln says, putting an arm on my shoulder, "because those can get messy and make things complicated, but it's not against the rules."

"He did say Hurley can't ask Presley out, if it makes you feel better," Eli says. Lincoln snorts, and Hurley punches him in the arm.

I huff out an annoyed sigh even though I should be grateful that they've worked all this out for me. "So." I fold my arms. "I just tell her that I've caught feelings?"

Eli puts a hand on my shoulder and grins at me. "Brock, have you ever heard of something called the grand gesture?"

CHAPTER 23
PRESLEY

Normally when I get home from work, I shed my work clothes quickly, put on sweats, pull my hair into a bun, and get comfy. If Brock and I were still just friends, I wouldn't change a thing about this routine. If I was still trying to convince Brock that I could just be his friend, I'd make myself as schlubby as possible to prove it to him.

But we've entered Operation Expose Brock, and I'm ruthless.

I can't be obvious, or he'll know immediately that something's up. So I choose a pair of leggings that does very nice things for my butt and a cropped half-zip hoodie that's the perfect amount of oversized. I happen to know this combo makes me look leggy. I take my hair down from the ponytail I wore all day today to keep it out of my face while I was working. There's a slight wave to it from the braid I wore on Tuesday, so it looks good without looking like I tried too hard. I touch up my make-up and hope that's not something Brock will notice—that my makeup looks fresh after a long day of work.

I am banking on the guy being oblivious to his own feelings for me, so I'm not too worried.

Next is setting the stage. I think Christmas spirit romance is the vibe to go with in this case. I spent any downtime I had today curating a Christmas love songs playlist and set it to play softly in the background. I make sure the lights to my Christmas tree are on and dim the main lights just enough to give the room a glow. I bought a special pie from Mila Delaford. Given who her brother is, and her circle of friends, apparently her maternity leave from her bakery has been filled with recipes for the football lifestyle. This pie has a light crust, isn't too sweet, and has some extra protein. Lincoln brought me a slice after they had Thanksgiving at their house, and I couldn't deny its deliciousness. (The things I heard about the banana cream pie she brought made me incredibly jealous. It obviously went quickly.) I want to provide a homey atmosphere for Brock to fall in love, and when you're talking about a guy who's six-seven, three-hundred pounds and in superb athletic shape, that's trickier than just making dinner.

I'm setting out the TOK book on the couch when my doorbell rings. My heart flutters, and I take deep breaths as I head toward the door and remind myself I'm playing a long game. Brock will realize his feelings eventually. He'll keep "messing up" and putting an arm around me or sitting close, and one of those times it's going to hit him.

"You got this," I whisper to myself before I open the door. "Hey!" I beam at him cheerfully as I swing it open. "Come in!" I turn from him, pretending not to notice the way his eyes slide over me, and leave the door open. Then I check over my shoulder on the pretense of pointing to the book and the couch to see if he's checking me out.

Yup. He hasn't said a word since he stepped inside, and the door is still standing open. We're calling this outfit a success.

"I got a pumpkin pie from Mila," I say when I get to the counter and turn to look at him. He quickly shuffles all the way in and shuts the door behind him, still blinking at me. "Like the one she brought to Thanksgiving."

"Oh?" he says, shoving his hands into his pockets. I force myself not to gloat over the detached way his voice sounds, as though he's coming back from a daydream. I've had a few of those myself, concerning him, so I won't judge him too much. Just for being a doofus when it comes to his own feelings. "That sounds great."

"Should we have a slice now or wait for a bit?" I grab dessert plates from the cabinet and turn to set them on the island to find him staring again. "Brock?" I ask when a few moments go by without him saying anything.

"Let's uh, wait for a bit." He plops down onto the couch. I do a victory fist pump in my head.

I leave the plates on the island and move over to the stove, where I have a couple mugs sitting next to it. "How do you feel about hot apple cider?" I ask as I fill the two mugs. "I'm trying to mix it up from hot chocolate." Especially since I noticed how little he drank the last time he was here. He doesn't do caffeine, I've discovered, and I bet he doesn't do a lot of sugar either. But I admire the way he still allows himself a small indulgence now and then despite his strict diet.

"Cider sounds great." He's picked up the book, and he plays with the bookmark I put in the other night after we read on the airplane. It came with the swag bag we got for getting tickets into the gathering with Gideon.

I bring the cider in on a tray and set it on the ottoman, pick up Brock's drink, and hand it to him. Then I take a seat on the couch next to him, crossing my legs to face him. I reach over to grab my cider and lift it up to take a sip. He watches me the whole time.

This is going so much better than I thought. My heart flutters again as I wonder if maybe our trip to New York has already helped Brock realize some things. Whatever the case, the ball is in his hands. And maybe, as a lineman, that's tough for him because he's not used to it.

"So, there's something I need to ask you before we start reading," I say after I put my mug down. "I need a favor."

Brock's expression is unreadable, but everything has gone so well so far, I don't worry too much. "You know I'll do whatever," he says.

I hold up a hand. On the off chance I've misread everything, I want to give him an out. Or at least the chance to keep things status quo until he figures out his feelings. "I know, but there's no pressure. And you're probably going to think I'm crazy."

Brock relaxes for the first time since he came into the apartment. He quirks an eyebrow. "Can anything get more crazy than Tuesday?"

"This? Maybe. I need you to go with me to the Westcott's Christmas Party, but you can totally say no."

He furrows his brows, but his eyes dance. "You *need* me to, but I shouldn't feel pressured to?"

"Absolutely."

He tilts his head. "Forgive me, but you're giving me mixed signals."

I'd panic about everything, except his expression is playful. This is like we were before I kissed him, and that means he's no longer overthinking everything he says to me. It could be because I stopped worrying so much, since I'm determined to make him admit his feelings. I'm still betting it's more though.

"I'm going to put the ring back. When we go to the West-cott's." I pick up my mug again and take another sip while I wait for his reaction.

His eyes widen. "That's it? That's the solution?" He leans toward me. "Did you figure out how she got it?"

I shake my head. "No, but Mrs. Westcott is terrorizing my parents' neighborhood, and I can't sit back anymore when I have it. Besides, their daughter is getting married on New Year's. They deserve to have the ring. I can't turn it in to the police because I don't know what will happen, but if it shows back up at the Westcott's house, they'll never link it back to Aunt Shannon."

He purses his lips, drawing my attention to them, but he

speaks before I can get too lost in thoughts about them. "But they could trace it back to you."

I've thought about that. I don't think there will be a way unless I'm caught with the ring in my possession. "I'll wear gloves."

A surprised laugh escapes him. "Of course I'll come with you, Pres. But what are you going to do? Crack the safe and slip it back in?"

I tip my head at him, feigning confusion. "Oh, is that hard?"

He eyes me but then grins. "Presley."

"I'll wrap it up like a gift. Westcotts have this huge tree in the middle of the room. We'll put it under the tree and bam! Christmas miracle."

"So you're the one Thornridge calls when he's planning Alden's heists," Brock deadpans.

I smack him on the shoulder and force myself to quickly pull my hand back from his muscled shoulder instead of caressing him the way I'd like to. "Simple is always best."

He studies me for a long time. "If you get caught, it's going to look bad. We could go to the police now. I'll back up your story."

I put my hand back on his arm, and not just because I want to feel the muscles again. This is allowed anyway. He put my hand here on Tuesday, so it's an allowed action, even if I weren't trying to prove a point.

"You weren't here when I opened the box. And besides, they'll say that's where I hid it after I stole it or something. I'm not going to get caught, Brock. There will be over a hundred people there. Besides, I'll have you as a distraction."

He looks down at my hand. I don't remove it immediately, and after a second, he puts his large, warm hand over mine. "So you do 'need' me," he says softly. I'd be a puddle at his sexy voice, but his eyes are dancing with mischief.

"I told you I did."

We stare at each other for another long moment before he draws back. "All right, Alden. Let's do this."

The way he's looking at me, the fluttering heart has vanished. It's thumping hard in my chest, and there's a good chance Brock can hear it. It feels like the tables have turned somehow, even though he's sitting with his back in the corner of the couch so he can face me, not touching me, but I still feel him like he's right up in my face.

I tap a finger on the book, even though keeping it together while he reads to me is going to be one of the most difficult things I do today. "Your turn to read."

Eli Dash has renamed this group "Former Best Friends Club."

Lincoln:

Hurley: Did your wife steal your phone?

Eli: No. Why?

Hurley:

Eli: Brock, I added my BIL, Landon.

Brock: Hey Landon.

Landon:

Landon: Eli, if you say anything about "friendzone to endzone," we will kick you out of the group.

Eli: Bro. I'm the founder.

Lincoln: Won't stop us.

Brock: I might let a few guys through on Sunday if you say that.

Lincoln:

Hurley:

Landon:

Eli: Brock, have you figured out your grand gesture yet?

Brock: Pretty sure Presley just handed it to me on a silver platter.

CHAPTER 24
BROCK

If the guys hadn't convinced me to do something big for Presley to make up for the way I shut her down when she kissed me, I would have told her last night. Kissed her about two seconds after I walked in the door. She gave me this look over her shoulder when she walked across the room that said she knew exactly why I was staring at her. She smirked.

Presley Tatum *smirked* at me.

She's gonna say, "I told you so," when I tell her how I feel. I deserve it.

So even though I wanted to admit everything and then have her snuggled in my arms while I read, I didn't. The guys are right that Presley deserves some magic. I can only imagine how she must have felt after I told her I didn't feel the same, and the courage it took for her to save our friendship after that humiliation. Besides, I've already decided she deserves the world.

There's a text waiting from Alexis Sterling when I get out of practice on Friday night.

Alexis Sterling: I chatted with Laura, who runs the Rays' social media. She's up to help you make some TOK videos to post to your account and the Rays' account. They love it.

Brock: You sure you need me? After what I found out on Tuesday, I think you know plenty of people on your own to get TOK movies made.

Alexis Sterling: Trying to back out?

Brock: I would never.

Alexis Sterling: Gideon refuses to use his other success for TOK. He wants it to make it on its own. Someone well known like you hyping it will push the success we got from the launch of book sixteen even further.

Brock: Then I'll definitely do my part. What you did meant the world to Presley.

Alexis Sterling: I'm glad you demanded. Gideon was very moved by his interaction with her. Looking forward to the videos.

Brock: 👍

Hopefully Laura will let Presley be in the videos too. We're hanging out again tonight to read, so I'll take a video and send it to my social media manager to post to my accounts.

Presley comes over to my suite at the hotel where I'm still staying. I haven't had a chance to find a place to live yet, which I need to do soon. I'm getting sick of living in a hotel. Lincoln and Layla have a couple extra rooms at their house, which they've offered to let me stay in if I want, but I need my own space.

Presley's wearing a pair of black joggers today with a Rays logo on the pocket. They fit her tighter than any pair of joggers I own, but I keep my perusal of them quick and turn my attention to her yellow Rays hoodie.

"You seem to have an endless supply of those."

"Bet you have a ton of Devils' gear."

We chat about the plans for the Christmas party next week—I'm meeting Presley at her apartment, where her parents will pick us up to take us to the party with them.

We settle on the sofa in the suite, and the setup isn't nearly as cozy as at her apartment with the Christmas songs, the tree, the pumpkin pie and cider, and the YouTube video with the crackling fire for ambience. At least I can pull that part off. I press play on the large TV in the room while she opens the book to find our spot. I've already texted her about making a video for social media tonight, so she sits next to me to make it easier, and once the video is recorded and sent off, she stays there.

She reads for about half an hour and then stops. It's been common for us, discussing the things happening for a few minutes before the reader moves on. But she doesn't say anything as she pushes the book into my lap.

"You'll need to read," she says.

I eye her. "Is your voice already tired?"

"No. I saw Kael's name on the next page. I won't be able to read their reunion." Her cheeks turn a deep shade of pink, and I nearly brush my fingers across them to feel the heat of her skin, to lean over and gently kiss each one. Sometimes the way I feel about Presley seems sudden. The spark I kept wondering about instantly bursting into a bonfire. Other times, my feelings are so natural and normal that I feel like the idiot the guys have implied I am for not seeing it sooner. I would do anything for her. I want to be with her always. I just didn't see it until I couldn't text her or call her after she kissed me—and even then it took time for me to understand what my missing her meant.

"I know it's stupid," she continues. "But I'm going to cry. I can already feel it."

I am so smitten with the way she loves these characters. They're like shared friends to us. I put my arm around her shoulders and pull her against me, taking the book in my other hand.

She huffs, and I furrow my eyebrows and look down at her. "What?"

"The way you can hold that in one hand is so unfair. That book has to be over a thousand pages long." The pink that hasn't left her cheeks deepens again. I would like to splay this hand across her back and press her to me. I stare at her, my brain contemplating the pros and cons of sticking with the plan I came up with for me to tell Presley how I feel at the Christmas party. Her parents are in on it at this point.

"Read the book, Brock," she says softly, her voice drawing me closer even though I shouldn't. Not yet.

There is no conceivable reason not to kiss her right now. I like her. I *really* like her, and I fall harder every minute I'm with her. Unless her feelings have changed in the last week, she likes me too.

I've almost convinced myself when my phone buzzes in my pocket. I look at the preview of the text on my watch.

Eli: How's it going? You laying down the foundation like we talked …

The rest of the text is hidden until I scroll. I quickly put my hand down. Yeah, you could say I've got the foundation well and started.

"Something you need to take care of?" Presley asks.

"Nah. Ready?" I mean that on so many levels. My reaction to her kiss could have scared her away completely. She might already be over me, although I don't think that's the case. She's sitting here, snuggling me … sure, you could argue this is a friend thing, but we've blurred the lines since Tuesday, and she knows it. But sticking with the plan for the night of the Christmas party is a good idea, just in case.

She nods at me, and I turn my attention to the book. By the time I get to the way Lyra and Kael run to each other, and how Lyra sobs into Kael's chest at seeing him alive and whole, tears are dripping down Presley's face. When she catches me glancing at her, she buries her face against my side.

"Pres," I say softly. "Gideon is good at this. No wonder he's a best-selling romance author."

She waves a hand around but doesn't pull her face from my side. "Keep reading."

I hold back my smile and tighten my arm around her. I put

my lips into her hair, take the briefest of inhales of the herbal scent, and kiss her quickly. If snuggling the way we are is blurring the lines, that was definitely a step over them. I can't gauge any reaction from Presley except that she might have stopped breathing.

That could be about her crying over the book. I turn my attention to the book, continuing with the scene, and a few pages later, after Lyra and Kael thoroughly kiss and then sit down to plan how they will sneak into the Palace of Azrion, Presley pulls her face from my side and sits up.

"You know what she means by 'I'll take care of the portal,' right?" I say, laying the book face down on the arm to take a few sips of the water bottle I set at the foot of the couch.

Presley points a finger at me. "No, Brock. It's not because she's the Obsidian Queen. It means she has a spell to get them through."

I put a hand up in fake surrender. "Whatever you say."

She huffs and pushes on my side. "She is not the Obsidian Queen." I only smile in response.

She takes the book back, and we read for another hour before we reluctantly stop since we both have to work in the morning. My day will be more chill than hers, with some meetings and then checking into a local hotel later. Even though it's a home game, the team stays in a hotel the night before to keep us focused and make sure we get the rest we need, along with it being a good way for the team to bond. All my friends' wives complain about not being able to come. Now I understand, considering I'd much rather be hanging out with Presley tomorrow night.

"I probably won't have a chance to talk to you until Monday, huh?" she says as she moves toward the door. I follow to make sure I get a goodbye hug.

Monday is the night of the Christmas party, so thankfully I don't have to do this much longer. "Meeting at your house at six."

"On the nose." She bobs her head at me as she reaches for the door handle. We're sliding quickly into awkward and that's the last thing I want. I reach over and pull her into a hug, fighting back every other temptation—like holding her for longer than a few seconds or tilting her chin back and pressing my lips to hers. Tuesday we were so effortlessly touchy that it's like I want to slide right past the new parts of a relationship where you question everything into a place where we're a couple who kisses goodnight. I guess that's what being friends first will do. I think of the way Lincoln swore it was the best way to go.

The night I met Presley, I was so drawn to her. Was it the necklace? Was it the way she smiled at me the first time I met her gaze? Did I start falling for her even then? I missed what's right in front of me because I focused so much on the little details. Details are my business on the field—what it means when a guy is lined up wrong, how the twitch of another lineman's arm can cue me in to where he might be moving. But I was so caught up in how I was supposed to feel about Presley on that detailed level—what a spark between us would feel like, if there was warmth where she touched me, how my stomach reacts to being near her—I missed the overall rightness of her in my life. The joy she brought. The craving of needing to be around her.

"Brock," she whispers. She's tilted her head away from me. Yeah, this hug has lasted way too long for just friends. Definitely too long for two people who are supposed to be focusing on *just being friends*.

I meet her eyes. She tilts her head slightly in a challenging way. She knows how I feel. Has she been waiting for me to see it, like the guys?

"I'll see you Monday," I say, not letting her go.

She arches an eyebrow at me. "I'll see you Monday."

I lean over and kiss her forehead. She knows, and she deserves the magic of me admitting I was wrong. *I told you so.*

Monday.

CHAPTER 25
PRESLEY

Everything has changed.

After Brock left my apartment Thursday night, the way he acted was all I could think about. Tuesday was one thing. We had a weird day, and he could have made excuses about how he treated me. He didn't, and it was like he took things up a notch.

And then Friday night? There was no more pretending we're just friends. No more watching everything he says and does. No more worry about leading me on.

He kissed my forehead.

He's done everything but tell me that he has feelings for me. I'm not sure what's going on, but I suspect the Former Best Friends Club has something to do with it, mostly because Eli, Lincoln, and Hurley, who's an honorary member because of his relationship with the other two, kept giving me knowing expressions every time they crossed my path at the game on Sunday.

Well those mischievous meddlers might have something up their sleeve, but tonight is my big play.

That is, the dress I'm wearing to the party. It's a shimmery green that I chose for Christmas vibes, but it gives off mermaid more than anything else with the way it hugs close to my knees and then flares out. The red high-heeled shoes I bought for the outfit give me four inches. A lot closer to Brock's lips, if you ask me. They have a ruffle on the toes that make them perfect for the festive Christmas look.

If Brock continues to pretend like he doesn't have more than "friendly" feelings toward me when he sees me in this dress, I have nothing left except to wear him down.

That's not a tactic I want to have to resort to.

My doorbell rings, and I wish I'd had Mom and Dad come here early so one of them could open the door and I could have a big, dramatic reveal. Instead I stride to the door, setting the tone for the confidence I need to confront Brock and prove my theory.

I pull open the door, leaving my hand on the handle and putting my other hand on my hip, striking what I hope isn't too obvious of a pose to show this dress off best I can.

"Hey," I grin, then I have to keep my own jaw from dropping. Brock's suit does some impressive things for him. Most offensive linemen carry weight in their middle. For them, it's all about being immovable mountains. Brock is the one that doesn't belong. He's strong and huge in his own right, but he's all muscle, looking more like a defensive tackle than an offensive lineman. This suit makes him look even sleeker. He's wearing all black from head to toe with a tie in the exact shade of green as my dress.

When I pull my gaze away from him, thinking how I've probably crashed and burned my plan by ogling him, I catch him still staring at me.

I can't help but smirk. "Your tie matches my dress," I say. My money is on the Former Best Friends Club being involved in this, though I couldn't tell you exactly how. I didn't tell any of them about my dress this week. We missed our usual Tuesday hang out, a.k.a. their therapy sessions, because I was in New York, and I haven't seen any of them most of the week except in passing at the facility and during the game.

Brock steps into the apartment. He stands close to me, and I don't increase the distance. "Lucky guess?" he says, looking down at me.

"Right ..." I keep my hand on my hip while I continue to eye him.

He smiles back at me. The air between us heats up. *Come on*, I coax him. *Just tell me. Better yet, kiss me.*

My phone rings from the couch. Probably my mom, letting us know they're here.

"Ready?" Brock asks. Neither of us has moved, and the door remains open. We're in a stand-off of some kind, neither one of us willing to totally break this moment between us.

The phone ringing forces me to be the one to step back. I hurry over to the couch to grab the phone. "Hey, Mom."

"We're downstairs. Whenever you're ready," she says. And then hangs up. I pull the phone from my ear and look down at it, frowning in confusion. That was weird.

"Everything okay?" Brock asks. He's closed the apartment door, but stands close to it, hands in his pockets, accentuating all those muscles. Arms, shoulders, trim waist.

I pull myself together. The point of inviting him tonight was to make sure he was looking at *me*. "No. My mom's being weird." I grab my red clutch from the couch and shove my phone in next to the small velvet box with a bow on it. If I put it under the tree, I want it to be recognizable quickly and not get overlooked tonight. Then I reach for the wrap in a shade of green just darker than my dress and drape it over my shoulders. "All ready," I say, walking back over to Brock. He watches me the whole way, so maybe we're even in our ogling score.

When we reach the sidewalk, Brock puts his hand on my back as we walk toward my parents' silver SUV parked right out front.

I suppress a shiver that has nothing to do with the cool temperature as Brock walks me around to the seat behind the driver's side. I almost laugh when I slide in and see that Mom has her seat pulled so far up that her knees are brushing the glovebox, leaving Brock plenty of room in the back seat.

I take the moment to slide even further in, making sure that when Brock takes his seat behind my mom that we'll be sitting right next to each other. If we're doing this couple thing without saying we're doing the couple thing, I'm going all in. Do I need an official declaration to be with Brock? Not necessarily. So long as whatever's going on tonight ends with a kiss.

Brock one ups me by draping his arm across the top of my seat the way he did when we drove to the airport. He doesn't comment, and this time he lets his hand drop close to my shoulder, fingers gently skimming back and forth over the fabric of my wrap. We chat with my parents on the drive back to their neighborhood, Brock and Dad quickly falling into football talk with Dad grilling Brock about how he sees so much on the line during the games. I hold tightly to my clutch, my fingers tracing the shape of the velvet box over and over. Mostly to keep my hand from finding its way to the top of Brock's thigh.

Then I realize we're basically in some weird game of chicken where we're waiting for the other one to break first. For one of us to point at the other and cry out, "Ha ha! I knew it! You like me." I lean forward to ask Mom if a friend of hers is coming to the party and put my hand on Brock's leg as I do, not moving it when I settle back into my seat after she answers. Brock doesn't look down at my hand, doesn't even react. My lips twitch. Despite wanting an answer now, this game is fun.

Mom glances at us over her shoulder. Dad goes back to talking about football.

Like every year, the Westcotts have a valet waiting to take the car, and a red carpet from the front drive to the entrance. They pay a photographer to take pictures since it's LA, and this party will have more than a handful of celebrities. The photographer's eyes brighten when she catches sight of Brock, and she motions for us to pause so she can get pictures. Perfect. I lean in close to

Brock and put one hand around his waist and the other on his chest.

Brock's move is to wrap his long arm around me and nudge me even closer. Touché, Brock, touché.

We enter through the tall, glass double doors of the Westcotts' mansion. Mr. and Mrs. Westcott are standing about midway through the large entry, greeting guests. Mrs. Westcott has on a placid smile as she says something to a couple who came in before us. Mr. Westcott's expression is tense, not exactly angry, but as though frustration is just under the surface. What's that about? Could he be regretting having their Christmas party as usual, considering what happened last year?

We reach the Westcotts, and Mrs. Westcott turns her placid smile on Mom. "Hello, Pam. Steven," she says. "Presley, wonderful to see you." She arches her eyebrows at Brock.

"This is my friend, Brock Hunter," I introduce.

Her expression never changes. "A pleasure, Brock." She extends a hand, which Brock shakes and then Mr. Westcott does the same without saying anything, just giving Brock a tight nod.

"As a warning," Mrs. Westcott says before we move away. "There are some gentlemen here tonight who will be asking questions. We would appreciate you giving them any information you can about the party last year. Trying to recover the ring, of course."

Mr. Westcott's jaw ticks, and I suspect his frustration is over Mrs. Westcott bringing private detectives to the party to grill the guests. I press my own lips together to keep from gasping or blubbering out a confession. This will mean extra eyes on me while I try to return the ring and I don't know if I'm a good enough actor if I get questioned.

"We're happy to help in any way we can," Mom assures her. Dad hums in agreement, and we move forward. Before we're out of earshot, I hear Mrs. Westcott imparting the same warning to the guests who came in behind us.

"Change in plan?" Brock asks lowly. "Considering we know now that she has some kind of security team onsite?"

I shake my head. "No way. Tonight is the night. I'll be extra careful."

He draws in a breath. "Extra careful doing what, Pres? You haven't told me how we're doing this."

"Keeping it simple," I say, tamping down my nerves. If Brock sees me scared in any way, he'll put a stop to this. Probably take the ring, march it up to Mrs. Westcott, and take whatever heat comes with it. I can't let him do that. "We'll admire the tree," I go on. "You block any view while I set it down, then we walk away casually." I shrug, but my stomach twists. This will be easy. Besides, I didn't do anything except find the ring in a box.

Everything will be fine.

I look up at Brock, and his steady gaze warms me, replacing the twisting in my stomach.

"Simple," he repeats. He slides his hand into mine and holds my gaze. His eyes go soft.

"Checkmate," I whisper.

He tilts his head. "What?"

I lean into him. "What's going on, Brock?"

He brushes a curl from my cheek. "Trust me."

I open my mouth to tell him that my feelings haven't changed, if anything they've grown, and I'm sure he feels the same. That I'm going to kiss him and put us both out of our misery, but it all dies in my throat at the way he's looking at me. The intensity of his gaze could burn right through me. It sends shivers across my skin, leaving goosebumps prickling on my arms. My knees even go a little wobbly.

"Okay."

Keeping hold of my hand, he leads me into the party and straight to the tree. I'm with him. I want to get this ring out of my possession and enjoy the rest of the night. We stand together, staring at it, pretending to admire the decorations and the millions of little lights on it. It's huge. Over fifteen feet, at least. A sparkling silver tree skirt is rumpled artfully around the bottom.

Both of our gazes dart across the crowd, looking for the "gentlemen" that Mrs. Westcott warned us about. "Clear?" he says, but it sounds like a question.

I don't see anyone suspicious looking. Would these guys stand out? Or has Mrs. Westcott thrown around enough cash that they'll be good at blending in. I summon all my confidence. "Clear," I say, even though I'm anything but sure about that.

I unzip my clutch and pull the velvet box out, cupping it in my hand. Brock steps behind me and I crouch, setting the velvet box down.

I stand quickly, and Brock puts his arms around me from behind, as though we've been standing like this the whole time. He kisses the side of my head, like he did on Friday night when we were reading and I was crying. It's the most comforting thing even though it shouldn't be. The touch of his lips should send my heart rate rocketing out of control. The softness of them, the smell of his cologne, pine and oranges, the way his lips shift my hair.

And yet, it makes me feel safe.

I stare down at the box, surprising disappointment filtering through me at the thought of walking away and leaving it there. Even if I'd kept it, I may have never known how Aunt Shannon got it. There's too much about her I'll never know, and maybe that's why I couldn't just hand this over to the police as soon as I found it. It represents all the little things. I swallow back emotion because this isn't the place I want to break down over the years I lost. Brock tightens his arms around me, and I squeeze gratefully where I'm holding onto them.

A moment later he lets me go, and we step away from the tree, hand in hand.

There's a string quartet this year providing the music, but it's all instrumental covers of popular songs. When we first came in, it was an Arianna Grande cover, but they've switched to "Last Christmas," slowed down in a way that somehow works.

"Let's dance?" Brock asks.

"Of course."

He leads me to the middle of the room, where several other couples are also swaying. I catch sight of my parents talking to another couple from their neighborhood, the Beaumonts, I think. I've met them a time or two when Dad has a barbecue. Mom winks at me. I raise my eyebrows at her, but she turns back to Mrs. Beaumont without acknowledging my reaction.

New guess: Brock knew the color of my dress because my mom told him. How did the meddlers get my parents involved in this? And what do they have up Brock's sleeve?

As he slides his arm around my waist and takes my hand in his, I forget why I care. As long as Brock's in on it—and judging from how close he's pulled me to him, Brock's in on it—it doesn't matter. If it includes kissing Brock under the mistletoe, I approve. I peer around the room, hoping to find some, and notice that the silver tree skirt is clear of any gifts, especially ones in black velvet boxes.

That's unnerving. Well, it's probably good that someone found it quickly. I think. I swallow. It's over, and I should be relieved. Sadness pricks at my chest, but it's the same questions. How did Aunt Shannon get the ring? Why did she leave it to me? Did I do the right thing by giving it back? I mean, of course I did, but is that what Aunt Shannon meant for me to do? Maybe once the Westcotts announce the ring is home safe and sound, more answers will start popping up.

A random confession from the thief that includes breaking into Aunt Shannon's and stashing it in a storage container? A girl can hope.

The Christmas song ends, and the quartet starts playing another song. The violin's melody is somehow familiar, but I can't place it right off.

"Follow me." Brock pulls me through the crowd toward the stage where the quartet is set up.

"What's going on?" I ask, but Brock just smiles, the way he has been all night.

When we get right up to the front, he puts his hands on my shoulders. "Stand right here."

"Miss Tatum?" a voice says, making Brock look up. I turn to look behind me. A man in an official-looking suit, not a sleek party suit like all the other men at the party, stands there, eyeing me. One of the gentlemen Mrs. Westcott was talking about?

My stomach drops. I know way more than I should, and I'm not comfortable talking to someone about the party last year given where the ring ended up. Is there any way to get out of this?

"Yes?" I ask politely.

"I need you to come with me please," he says in a low voice.

Brock steps in. "I know Mrs. Westcott wants you to talk to all the guests, but can this wait until later?"

"No, Miss Tatum. We need to speak to *you* right now." The way he emphasizes that has me thinking this could be more than just relaying what I know about last year. But how? We slipped the box under the tree quickly and naturally.

I think it's best to act innocent until proven otherwise. "Is something wrong?" I ask. I hope my confused face looks convincing.

"Please come with me." He moves to take my elbow to escort me out, I assume, but Brock blocks his hand, putting an arm protectively around my waist.

"We'll answer your questions later." Brock's expression is impassive, but his resting face is … intimidating. It reminds me of that glare I thought he was giving me at Lincoln's wedding when he was just concentrating on my necklace. I'm pretty sure he means for *this* expression to be threatening.

The guy forces a smile, but he doesn't cow. "You're welcome

to enjoy the party. We need to have a quick word with Miss Tatum. Now."

Brock's expression narrows. "I go where she goes."

The man hesitates and then finally says, "Follow me." He leads the way back the way we came into the party. I make sure not to look over at the tree, and Brock doesn't say anything as we exit. Before we leave the ballroom, I glance over my shoulder at the last place I saw Mom. She isn't there, but a quick scan shows her and Dad not very far away talking to someone else. Mom furrows her eyebrows at me, but I give a quick shake of my head and force a calm expression for her. I definitely don't want her getting involved in this.

The security guy takes us back to a small office off the entry foyer. Inside is a makeshift security office like you might see on a TV show. I've only been in the Westcotts' house once, outside of the Christmas parties I've attended, but I think last year it was a regular office. There's a computer on the desk with two large screens, and another man in a suit like the one who led us here sits in front of it, scanning feeds from all over the house. I flush when I see that between three different camera angles trained on the ballroom, it has full coverage of the tree. I swallow but turn to look at the security guy standing in front of us with that same confused look. Everyone knows they're here to ask questions, and for now, I'm going to pretend that their intense interest in me doesn't have something to do with the box I left under the tree. Maybe there's a chance they're going to ask me if I saw anything because I'm on camera near the tree. I cross my fingers, hoping that something blocked me when I set the box down.

The first security guy holds a hand out to a straight-backed chair in one corner. "Would you like to take a seat, Miss Tatum?"

"What's going on?" I repeat before moving. Someone who's innocent would be getting nervous about that by now. Lucky for me, the nervous part is easy to portray given that I am indeed nervous.

"We'd like to ask you a few questions about the box you left under the tree." He gestures to the chair.

I take one more stab that they're bluffing because Brock and I were in the area around the time the box appeared. "Box?"

The security guy lets out a breath that sounds like a laugh. "Booker," he says to the guy at the computers. The computer guy taps a bunch of buttons and on one of the screens a video comes up. The camera shows very clearly me and Brock walking up to the tree. It's from the side, so when Brock stands behind me, it hides nothing. You see me crouch, put the box down, and then stand back up to Brock wrapping his arms around me.

My face is completely on fire.

"I made her do it," Brock says.

"Don't even start with that." The last thing he needs in his career right now is to get mixed up in this. "He had nothing to do with it. Don't listen to him. Make him leave."

The security guy eyes us both. Brock is scowling hard core now. "Presley."

"He had nothing to do with this," I insist.

"What is 'this'?" the security guy asks.

I'm not dragging Aunt Shannon into it either. Not without knowing more than I do. "I found the ring"—Security Guy scoffs, like I knew he would—"and I knew no one would believe me." How did I not consider the fact that the ring was stolen from this very party last year, so obviously the Westcotts upped security? Given all the things Mrs. Westcott has done recently, and especially the warning we got at the beginning of this party, I should have foreseen this. Did I really convince myself it was just a couple PIs asking questions?

"I wanted to return it."

There's a tap at the door, and Security Guy steps away from me to open it. Standing outside is a policeman.

My entire body goes cold.

CHAPTER 26
PRESLEY

This wasn't how I pictured the night going, to be honest.

Maybe because I deluded myself into thinking that it was going to be that easy to put the ring under the tree and walk away and everyone would be happy. And I didn't think past returning the box. There was the theoretical possibility I'd get in trouble, but I didn't imagine things like a police station and sitting in an interrogation room in my Christmas party dress.

Most of my imaginations for this night included Brock's jaw dropping to the ground when he saw me in my dress. (I think I did accomplish that at least.) Some dances where I didn't hold back on the romantic touching to prove to Brock he has feelings for me. The culmination of the night being a kiss under the mistletoe and Brock admitting he was wrong.

The policeman who brought me to the station half an hour ago didn't even ask me anything when he stuck me in this room. Are they sweating me out? Like a detective's going to show up here soon, and I'll be so overwrought that I'll end up confessing right out of the gate?

I would be happy to confess! Only I don't have anything to confess to except possession of stolen property. Is that a felony?

I'm so getting fired over this. I drop my head onto the table. What a waste of a dress.

Brock wanted to come to the police station with me, but Officer Morgan said he couldn't ride in the police car even though Brock kept saying he was in on the whole thing.

I kept countering it by telling Officer Morgan that Brock was only saying that to protect me, and Brock glared at me every time I said it.

There's a tap on the door, and I raise my head as it opens, expecting Officer Morgan or a detective in a suit like in all the crime shows on TV to walk in. But it's neither. I squint, as though I must be seeing things because of the stress of all this.

"Thomas?" I blink a few more times, trying to convince my brain that my aunt's boyfriend is striding into the room and taking a seat across from me. "Oh, my gosh," I say in a rush, my eyes widening. "I'm in really big trouble. They've brought in the FBI?"

Thomas puts a hand on my arm as I start to hyperventilate. "No one brought in the FBI, Presley," he says in a calm voice. "I'm here to help you."

I let out a whoosh of breath and take his hand in mine, squeezing. "Oh, thank you so much. I guess Brock could probably throw some money around, or my parents, but I didn't want to get them involved."

"You're not being arrested. Not once I explained what had really happened to the ring." He chuckles.

I pause at the calm way he's handling this, and a million things run through my head, loudest of all that Thomas has the answers I thought I'd never get. But also how much I've missed him. We text from time to time, but he has a very busy job, and I know by the stories he's told that he sometimes works undercover. In the three years that he and Aunt Shannon dated, there were at least four times she had to go multiple days, and a couple weeks in one instance, without talking to him at all. He's younger than Aunt Shannon by a few years, and his profession has kept him in good shape. There are lines around his bright blue eyes, but they feel like they come more from how much he enjoys life than anything else. He has a sprinkling of grays over his head, a sprinkling I saw disappear a couple times over the years I knew him, thanks to operations he was working on. He's a good-looking guy, but Aunt Shannon used to talk all the time about his kind eyes. He was her hero, and he was smitten with her. Watching them fall in love was what I imagined it would have been like to see my parents fall for each other. Seeing the times Thomas would look at her like he could memorize her or like he would never get enough broke my heart almost as much as losing her did. And I feel it all over again right now as he stares down at me, all the same memories probably sliding through his mind too.

"Hey, Thomas," I say, since I didn't really greet him before. My throat tightens.

"Hey, Pres." He squeezes my hand this time, and we sit there, just feeling for a moment.

Finally, I have to ask. "So about that ring?" I arch an eyebrow at him.

He lets go of my hand and sits back in his chair. "The ring isn't just some priceless family heirloom. It's a major art piece, since it was created by some hot shot, European jewelry designer in the 1800s especially for the Westcott family. It's also worth three million dollars."

My jaw drops, and then my body goes cold again like it did when the security guys at the Westcott's house showed me the video of me caught red-handed. "I had a three-million-dollar ring sitting in a storage box in my closet for a year?" The questions start spinning again. What if someone had known that Aunt Shannon had it? How long would it have been before they tracked it down to me? I put a hand to my forehead.

Thomas snorts. "Sounds like it was pretty safe."

"How did it get there?" I blurt.

"I stole the ring." He sighs. "I was undercover with the small heist crew, just a couple guys who were going to sell the ring to some bigger dealers we were after."

"*You* stole it!" Lightness bubbles up, maybe a release of all the stress over the last hour. I'd even considered that he might've been the one who stole it, but it hadn't occurred to me it would have been as part of something official. "Oh my gosh, Thomas," I exclaim. "You teased Aunt Shannon about being suspected, and you literally had it. How did you get through the search?"

"Put the ring in a secret pocket in my suitcoat. I had a ring box on hand to put it in once we were out." His tone is all *just a regular day on the job*. "Anyway, I made sure the crew knew I was connected with someone who could get me into the party and talked my way into being the safecracker and bagman, since the crew was small."

I hold up a hand. "Wait. If the ring was worth so much, why didn't the Westcotts have the same security like they had this year? They just searched us all when it came up missing."

Thomas frowns. "They had cameras and everything. They do every year. But we were professionals, and I had the FBI on my side."

I shake my head. "I feel so stupid."

Thomas laughs. "I hope it deters you from a life of crime, if anything."

"I promise." I tilt my head at him. "So then you hid it at my apartment because …?"

He swallows, the amusement draining from his expression quickly. "When Shan and I got home from the party, she found the ring box in my jacket. She didn't know the ring was famous or anything, and I hadn't told her about my undercover assignment. She thought …" He clears his throat. "She thought I was going to propose. We'd tabled the proposal discussion when she got her diagnosis—her idea."

"I know." We were all aware that Thomas and Aunt Shannon were arguing over getting married, that she insisted she wouldn't saddle him with an invalid so he could play nursemaid in her last years. "But how come she didn't recognize the ring?" I knew what it was the moment I found it.

"I don't know if you remember, but the Westcotts didn't tell us at the party what had been stolen—just said something of great value to them. The family and the police didn't release that it was the Christmas Ring until … later."

Meaning, after Shannon had died. She never knew what she had.

"She …" He pauses, closing his eyes as he tries to compose himself, but his words come out soft anyway. "She was excited. And then she pretended to get mad about me ignoring her wishes, and I didn't have the heart to tell her what the ring was for, because I had to argue with her about letting me take care of her." He clenches his fist on the table, his frustration with her evident. And that must be complicated to deal with along with the grief. Mom and Aunt Shannon got into a couple arguments about Thomas, about Aunt Shannon pushing him away after her diagnosis. One of the few times I heard my mom raise her voice to Aunt Shannon was to tell her how stupid she was being, that Thomas loved her, and he was a good man. Then Mom had gasped, started crying, and pulled Aunt Shannon into her arms.

I can still hear their voices, their sobs, when Aunt Shannon cried that she couldn't do this to him.

Tears run down my cheeks now in earnest. It feels as fresh as the day Mom called, crying so hard she couldn't get the words out and Dad had to take the phone to tell me Aunt Shannon was gone. "She was so stubborn," I whisper.

He nods, but he doesn't go on yet. I reach across to him again with both hands, and he puts his in mine. Finally he clears his throat. "The next morning, the guys on the heist crew we thought were small-time got caught up with some terrorists, and I ended up on a flight to Albania. Everything happened fast—the addition of terrorists to the case had pushed the ring completely out of my mind, and the FBI thought I'd handed it off to my partner already. My partner thought I had it with me to play my part. By the time we realized everything, Shannon was gone. And so was the ring." He lets out a long, resigned breath. "The only explanation we could come up with was that another player we weren't aware of tracked me and Shannon home and stole it after I left. FBI forensics combed over the scene, making sure it was nothing more than an accident." He shrugs. "I don't know why she put it in your box, Presley. That's the only thing I don't know."

I think back to the morning that Mom found Aunt Shannon. She had fallen sometime the night before. When Mom couldn't get a hold of Thomas right away, she'd called the FBI. He'd gotten home late that night, and as I think back to the fear in his eyes then, it makes sense. He'd thought his job had gotten Shannon killed.

"It *was* an accident?" I say to confirm they didn't find out anything later.

"Yeah. No sign of anyone else playing a part, and everything lined up with what seemed to have happened."

In other words, Aunt Shannon lost her footing, thanks to the ALS beginning to rob her of her strength in her limbs, and fell headfirst into her wooden coffee table, knocking her out, giving her a massive brain bleed that killed her within hours since she couldn't call for help. Mom agonized for months after Aunt Shannon's death about all the things she should have done, things they'd talked about for the future. Aunt Shannon's diagnosis was less than a year old. They thought they had time to think about a caregiver who checked on her regularly or moving in with Mom and Dad.

Thomas and I sit in silence, both of us remembering the days that followed Aunt Shannon's death and the shock that reverberated through us. Mom would say things like, "She hated the idea of us having to take care of her like she was a baby," trying to find some sliver of comfort in what had happened, and it never worked.

"Well," I say, breaking the silence. "That all means we know one thing, Thomas."

He squints at me, his eyebrows coming together. "And what is that?"

"She was definitely going to say yes."

He pats my hand, tears in his eyes, and then pulls away. "Let's get you out of here. There's a *very* large man out there threatening all kinds of things, and we should avoid him getting arrested if we can."

I blush. "He had nothing to do with this," I say for good measure. Despite the fact that I'm basically innocent in all of this and Thomas can prove it, Brock and I still concealed stolen property, and who knows what other crimes. If Brock annoys LAPD enough, they might decide to charge him with something.

Thomas chuckles. "Sure, Pres. Sure."

CHAPTER 27

BROCK

So much for grand gestures.

I have at least ten text messages from the Former Best Friend's Club asking how my planned serenade to Presley went, and each one is increasingly desperate. Eli is now sending commiserating texts, telling me he gets how it feels to be rejected, since he thought Court had rejected him, and he's coming up with a plan. I haven't answered any of them. How do I explain that before I could even start singing, Presley got arrested for stealing a priceless family heirloom that turned out to be worth over three million dollars?

When Presley told me about her plan, warning bells rang in my head but I ignored them. I thought I was being dramatic, and the Christmas party would be the perfect opportunity to tell Presley I have feelings for her in a big way to make up for rejecting her.

I'm driving Presley to her apartment now, where I'm going to tell her the truth about how I feel and kiss her for a while.

That sounds like a perfect grand gesture right about now.

At least I'm holding her hand, and she hasn't said anything.

"You okay?" I ask. She's been quiet most of the drive.

She smiles over at me. "Yeah. Seeing Thomas brought up a

lot of stuff about when Aunt Shannon died. Just contemplative." She holds up our hands, which have been enjoined on the console. "Is this us just being friends?"

I chuckle. "No, but let's get you home and then talk?" I don't want to make this confession in the car, while I'm driving, when I can't end it with a kiss. My grand gesture has been ruined, but I'm hoping to salvage at least part of it.

She eyes me. "Good talk?"

How she can wonder that at this point, I don't know, but I have been purposefully vague about our relationship status. "Good talk," I assure her.

She leans her head over to rest it on my arm, then she dials her parents on speaker phone. She's texted them that she's fine and headed home, and they know the story from Agent Stahl. He told me to call him Thomas, but I can't bring myself to. He knew before her parents did that Presley had been arrested and told them not to come down to the police station, that he would handle everything. I should have gone and talked to them as soon as the policeman took Presley outside, but I was sprinting out to get the car from the valet to follow the police car since they wouldn't let me ride with her. Luckily, the valet let me take the Tatums' vehicle, and someone from the party gave them a ride home, since they just live a few blocks away from the Westcotts.

"My mom will sleep better if she hears my voice," Presley whispers to me as the phone rings.

Her mom answers before I can say anything. "Why didn't you *tell me* she left you the ring?" she says instead of hello.

Presley sighs before she answers. "I knew you'd tell me to turn it in, and I wanted to figure out a way to return it without getting Aunt Shannon in trouble."

Mrs. Tatum huffs. "Shannon called me that night." Her voice gets tight. It would have been one of the last times she'd spoken to her sister. From my conversations with Presley, I know that her aunt died the next evening sometime. "She told me Thomas had a ring, that she'd seen it. We argued, because I told her to accept it. She said she was thinking about it." She pauses, and Presley squeezes my hand. I don't know if she even realizes it. "She said she was putting it in Thomas's box to make sure it was safe, and they'd talk about it when he got home."

"Then how did it get in my box?" Presley asks.

"I don't know, sweetie. But she was having episodes with her eyesight too, and when I got the boxes from her closet, yours and Thomas's were next to each other. She probably mixed them up." I hear a long intake of breath from Mrs. Tatum. Presley's eyes were red and puffy when she emerged from the interrogation room with Agent Stahl. I think this whole family has been reliving those awful hours after Shannon Cox died suddenly. "If you had just told me ..." Mrs. Tatum finally sighs.

"Honestly," Presley says, "I should have called Thomas to ask for his advice, and then everything would have been fine."

Mrs. Tatum laughs. "So, you're okay?"

"I'm fine, Mom. I'm going home to sleep ... probably." Presley tilts her head to look up at me. I shrug, trying not to smile. Her going to sleep isn't in my plans. Not for a little while, at least.

"You with Brock?" Mrs. Tatum asks.

"Yeah, he's driving me."

"Mmmm, okay. I'll talk to you tomorrow then."

"Love you, Mom."

"Love you, sweetie." Mrs. Tatum's voice breaks a little, and then the call clicks off.

"Seems that telling my mom I was with you ended that call a lot sooner than I expected ..." She sits up to eye me.

"Interesting."

"My parents were in on whatever was going on tonight, weren't they?"

I laugh but don't say anything else.

"You're going to tell me, right? What you were about to do when the police hauled me off?"

We're stopped at a traffic light, so I lean over and kiss the top of her head. "I promise."

———

WHEN WE GET to Presley's house, I tell her to stay in her dress and then sit her on one of her kitchen island stools in the middle of her living room. Thanks to Landon, I have "For the First Time," the karaoke version, cued up on my phone. The texts have quieted from the group for now, but there are several unread messages that I scrolled past. The guys are begging for information on the night. When I asked for the link to the song, that quieted them. I'll have to fill them in but they've obviously deduced that all is not lost yet.

I take a few steps back from Presley. I don't sing often in front of people, not since I was younger for church or school, but my voice is good enough for this. That's why we settled on this particular grand gesture. I start the song. She squints in concentration as the notes play, probably trying to place where she knows it from.

I come in, singing softly, the words about seeing someone in a way you didn't before. By the time I'm to the chorus, I've come to stand next to her, taking her hand, and pulling her up from the stool to dance with her.

"Brock," she says breathily. "Your voice …!"

I smile at her and continue singing. She stares up at me, awe and amusement playing across her face. When I get to the second verse, she rests her head against my chest, and we sway as I sing the rest of the song to her.

When it ends, we keep swaying, and since I'm not by my phone to pause the music, it keeps playing. Another instrumental pop song comes up, but it doesn't matter. I'm holding Presley in my arms and it's perfect. Maybe better than if I'd been able to sing to her in front of everyone at the Christmas party.

I'm the one who leans back and tilts her chin up toward me. "I was dumb, Presley."

She smiles. It's mischievous and triumphant. She's obviously known all along—not just her feelings for me, but my feelings for her. "You like me?" she teases.

"I like you," I confirm, lowering my face toward hers.

We stop swaying. Presley's hands cup my cheeks, and she tilts her head the perfect angle for our lips to meet. As they melt together, I wonder what I missed that first time, how I didn't understand that this warmth and familiarity were mixed with the fire that roars to life. It was smoldering under the surface all along. My hands slide down to her hips, and I pull her closer to me the same time she wraps her arms around my neck. When her fingers slide into my hair, my knees go weak.

I remember the reunion kiss between Lyra and Kael that we read a few nights ago, the way Kael lifted Lyra up to him and then spun her around in his joy at seeing her again, safe and whole. Presley would definitely appreciate that move.

I wrap my arms around her back and lift her, spinning her slowly around, and grinning against her lips. Our kiss breaks as she laughs and tilts her head back.

"A perfect reenactment," she says, leaning toward me again. I don't set her down as we kiss again. After a few moments, she giggles.

"Are you trying to show off how strong you are?" she asks, placing her hands on my upper arms.

"Is it working?"

She runs her hands down my arms then back up and along my shoulders until she's cupping my face again. "Brock Hunter, you are massive. Showing off your muscles isn't necessary." She leans over me to kiss me again.

Finally I set her down. "Want to change into something comfy and we'll read?"

She shakes her head, still leaning into me. "I mean, I do want to get comfy, but let's drink some hot cocoa, eat some Christmas cookies, and watch *Diehard*."

"It's going to take us forever to finish the book at this rate." I don't let go of her waist.

"Says the guy who suggested we read it together. Besides, I don't mind how long it takes." She grins at me.

"You're just afraid of finding out that Lyra is, in fact, the Obsidian Queen."

She shoves against my chest. "She is not."

I nudge her toward her bedroom. As breathtaking as she is in that dress, it can't be comfortable. Besides, she's as hot to me in a pair of leggings and a hoodie. She leans up and kisses me quickly on the lips, smiling as she pulls away, and then heads for her room.

"Are you going to go back to the hotel and change?" she asks, pausing in the doorway of her bedroom. I can't help but take one last look at her toned muscles and gorgeous curves shown off in that shimmery dress. I shrug out of my suit coat. My dress shirt is stretchy and not uncomfortable, so I pull my tie loose and unbutton the top button. Her cheeks flood with pink, and it's my turn to smirk at her.

"I'm not going anywhere."

EPILOGUE

PRESLEY

To: gideon.thornridge@obsidiankingdom.com
From: ptatum@larays.com
Gideon,
I was absolutely not ready for that.
Presley Tatum

Before I can ring the bell, Brock opens the door of his condo in Malibu, backpack slung over his shoulder. He grins when he sees me and lets the backpack slide to the ground to scoop me into his arms. Though he was obviously on his way out the door to head to the hotel for the night, he doesn't hurry as he greets me with a long, lingering kiss that makes my toes curl, even after a full month of dating. Sometimes our relationship feels like we've been together forever—the same way our friendship felt after only a couple weeks. Sometimes he kisses me and it's as electric as the first time. The way he can completely wrap me up in his arms, and how small and protected I feel against his massive chest—I melt over it on a regular basis.

"Thought you were going to miss me, and I wouldn't see you until the game tomorrow," he murmurs into my hair after we pull away from each other.

"Traffic sucked. Sorry." I rest my head against his chest.

"Drive to the hotel with me?" he suggests, nodding toward the SUV at the sidewalk. He always takes one to the hotel so he doesn't have to figure out how to get his car home, unless I drive him or he goes with Eli Dash, who lives close by. "I'll pay Carl for the drive, and you can take me," Brock says, taking my hand to lead me down the sidewalk. He gives some cash to the driver, who thanks him and pulls away, then we head to my car. It's definitely not as luxurious as the Escalades that Brock always hires (and drives one of his own), but at least it's not a tiny sedan he needs to squeeze into. Thankfully, I drive a Toyota Sequoia, and he won't be too cramped.

I pause next to the passenger door before he gets in. "I brought you something in case you get bored tonight." I hold out the latest romcom by Gideon Thornridge, which is how I always think of this author, no matter the name on the book. I just finished it. This one is already optioned for a miniseries, according to Mom. Brock and I have been working our way through his pretty expansive backlist since I quit reading *Veil of the Queen* a couple weeks ago when it turned out that Brock has been right all along. It's a testament to the fine man he is that he hasn't finished reading it himself or pressured me to finish it with him so we can see how Gideon has justified this complete betrayal. So instead, we're reading his romcoms, and I love it as much as if I'd discovered them with Aunt Shannon herself.

"How was it?" Brock asks, taking the book and slipping it into his backpack.

"Well, no betrayals and the kiss scene was *mwah*." I imitate a chef's kiss. "Perfection."

"There are going to be TOK movies." Brock leans over the top of the SUV as I walk around to get in. "You going to finish *Veil* before then?"

I shrug and open my door. "I'm going to have plenty of time to decide."

Brock chuckles and slips inside.

We chat about another romcom as we drive, the one that Brock just finished and that I read right before him. He doesn't hate these books, but he's such a good sport to read them with me. It melts my heart every time he sends me a quote from one and comments with something like, "Just like you," when it's a description of a beautiful woman, or "I know exactly how he feels," when a guy is pining after the love interest. That always makes me snort.

When we pull up into the circular drive of the hotel, Brock gets out and makes his way over to my side, so I get out of the car to hug him goodbye. I'll see him tomorrow on the sidelines, but we won't get to talk much since we're both focused on our jobs. Still, I'll miss hanging out with him tonight. I always do.

"Good luck," I say as he leans down to kiss me goodbye.

"I've had the best luck since meeting you," he murmurs against my lips.

"Helps that you're on a good team now," I tease.

He pulls back enough to look me in the eyes. "Helps now that I have someone I want to be the best man I can for."

"I think you should definitely keep reading these romance books. They're rubbing off."

He grins and leans over to kiss me again. "Helping me put to words what I feel," he whispers. "But there's one thing I don't need help with." He cups my cheek in his hand and studies me.

"And what's that?"

"I love you Presley Tatum. That's what."

The words don't come as a shock, but they send a whirlwind of feeling through my body anyway. I throw my arms around his neck, and he puts his around my waist, hugging me and pulling me off my feet. I laugh softly as I press my face into the hollow of his neck and kiss him there.

"I love you too, Brock Bennett Hunter," I whisper against his ear. We hug like this for several moments, and then he sets me down. He slips his hand under the Obsidian Kingdom necklace I wear more often than not these days and leans over to kiss it too.

"Also definitely my good luck charm," he says winking at me. "Since it lured me to you." He kisses me on the cheek and then straightens, letting out a little sigh that means he hates he has to leave me. It happens a lot, and it's very endearing.

I hold the necklace and wave at him as he rounds the front of the SUV and makes his way into the hotel. I think Aunt Shannon has been matchmaking all along, and I can't help but be grateful.

I get back in my car and watch Brock until he disappears through the doors, giving me one last wave before they slide closed behind him.

"Thanks, Aunt Shannon," I whisper.

———

Would you like a bonus epilogue of Brock + Presley, and your favorite
LA Rays players and their wives?
Download Here

ACKNOWLEDGMENTS

First off, to everyone who loved *Mistletoe Kisses & Something Merry* last year, because there would not have been four books in this series if not for that book taking off and everyone wanting Layla's story. It turned the sweet characters in *Best Friends, Backups & Something More* from a novella meant to be a one-off into a set of beloved characters. To all my readers: I say it often because it's so true. I would not be here with *you.*

To my critique group: Kaylee Baldwin, Kate Watson, Jen Atkinson, Gracie Ruth Mitchell, and Susan Henshaw. I seriously know the coolest people. You found all the right things to make this book shine. To Kate, who did a full beta read for me and pushed me to work, as usual, for this book to be its best. And to Kaylee, my dear friend, for her editing work in lightning fast time. Indie authors need people who can get stuff done, and my people get stuff done. To my Zoom sprint group, for keeping me on task (most of the time). You all make it feel like I have an office full of coworkers, and since I'm an extrovert, it really really helps.

To my family, for always being so supportive, both the Savages and the Clarks. To my sisters, who answer brainstorming questions and questions about slang to keep this elder millennial "bussin." To Savanna, who read very quickly for me to help me smooth out some rough spots. To my husband, for not complaining (too much) about me not cooking dinner, and to my boys for being generally oblivious to me. Makes working easy when you're not sure if you want to hang out with me anyway. But especially to my oldest son, who left on the mission in the middle of producing this book—that was super helpful. ;) But seriously, I love you all and your support of me and the job I love.

To my Heavenly Father. More often as the years go by I recognize that I could not do this job without You helping me—bringing amazing people into my life and blessing me with the right words. Thank You.

MORE FROM RANEÉ S. CLARK!

LA Rays Sports Romance
Best Friends, Backups & Something More
Mistletoe Kisses & Something Merry

Houston Pumas Sports Romance
The Comeback

Love in Little River
Roxy's Song
Dating Dry
Catching Coy
Hallie's Hero
Addy's Prince Charming
Battling Ben

Finding Taylor
Love in Little River Prequel Novella
(Free for newsletter subscribers!)

———

Playing for Keeps Series
Playing for Keeps
Double Play
Love, Jane
Meant for You

Historical Romance
Beneath the Bellemont Sky
The Heiress and the Boy Next Door
A Lady's Promise

Get a FREE novella!
Sign up for Raneé S. Clark news and get *Roxy's Song,* the first
book in the Love in Little River series for FREE!
SIGN UP HERE!

Thank you so much for reading Presley + Brock's story! If you
enjoyed the book, please consider leaving a review on Amazon.
Reviews are vital to the success of a book, so thank you!
Follow me on social media for news about my writing and more
football + Jane Austen books!

ABOUT THE AUTHOR

In a house overrun by boys, it shouldn't come as a surprise that Raneé loves football and enjoys watching (and playing!) other sports as well, like basketball and baseball. When she's not chauffeuring three busy boys to various activities (and sometimes while she is!), Raneé is either writing, reading (usually romance), obsessing over clothes in the form of her online boutique, or figuring out how to get a Crumbl cookie in rural Wyoming. When her real-life love interest can drag her away from imaginary worlds, she doesn't mind spending some time with him in the great outdoors that he loves.

You can find out more about Raneé's writing on Facebook and Instagram.

www.ingramcontent.com/pod-product-compliance
Lightning Source LLC
Chambersburg PA
CBHW071506140726
47997CB00005B/1873